The Clandestine Cookie Jar

by

Rick Burgess

This is a work of fiction. The resemblance of any character in this story to any person living or dead is purely coincidental.

for all those that dwell on the bottom

THIS PAGE INTENTIONALLY LEFT BLANK

One

It was a bitterly cold night, even for the middle of January. Ellen June Jung watched in the moonlight as her breath became a wispy fog each time she exhaled. Blowing a stream of air towards her forehead in frustration, she tousled the bangs that extended beyond the edge of the wrap that covered her head.

Ellen June walked in long gangly steps in the snow at the edge of the road, knobby knees and elbows swinging in time as if marching, a trait carried over from childhood, never outgrown. The freshly fallen snow had acquired a thin frozen crust that yielded just enough with each step to provide a negligible amount of traction that made her walking easier, almost effortless.

Muttering to herself, she continued towards her home on the outskirts of town. "If I catch that boy, I'm going to kill him!" Ellen said, finding comfort in the sound of her own voice which provided company along this abandoned stretch of road. To be sure, this was a non-serious threat to commit murder. Still, with tongue in cheek, she added, "I could get away with it, too! After all, I am an embalmer! The first female licensed in the state!" Her proud acknowledgment came with a smirk, for she knew that it was only her quirky personality that would allow her to harbor both feelings of love, and thoughts of murder, at the same moment.

Ellen's apprehension at times bordered on the irrational, and her search for this person who was the central joy of her life had only met with frustration, making her worry all the more. Yet, the overpowering love that she carried in her heart kept pushing her forward, even though her disappointment over the lack of success in this unfruitful search still remained.

"Gee," she finally found herself saying, "I sure hope he's all right!"

The person occupying Ellen June's thoughts was none other than her own seventeen year old son, Richie. He had been missing since the early afternoon when he failed to return home from a session of studying with his high school girlfriend, Susan.

A polite and respectful girl, she remained sweet and unaffected despite the rumors of her mother's reputation as a woman of dubious virtue. "The woman is a tramp!" Ellen said in an outward expression of disgust. "She's a real home wrecker! And Richie, especially, would be vulnerable, since it's likely that he has inherited his father's lascivious glands!"

In truth, though, Jon Jung, Ellen's husband, was ever faithful; of this she had no doubt. It just so happened that he also possessed a bawdy sense of humor that he was never afraid to exhibit. Probably developed, she reasoned, as a counterpoint to the solemn nature of his profession: funeral director.

Ellen could only hope that her son would resist the temptation of this alluring older woman, particularly in the setting that Richie's father had come to refer to as the town's "horizontal recreation area".

However, up to this point, Ellen had not even considered that Susan, and the possibility of youthful, healthy sex, might be just as much a fascination to the boy and his "glands" as was the girl's mother. Still, Ellen June had frequently requested that Richie and Susan do their studying together at the Jung's house.

Their house was the problem as far as Richie was concerned, for it happened to be situated just beyond the entrance gates to the town's cemetery. Richie's friends, for that reason, were rather reluctant to visit their home, especially after dark when the quiet of the graveyard was, perhaps, a little too disconcerting even for the brashest of youths. However, that didn't stop them from giving Richie a good natured kidding whenever the after school activities bus dropped him off in the early evening at the stop near the cemetery. Seeing Richie stepping from the bus, someone would say, "Ghoul night!" His only reply was, "Cute."

But Ellen felt that there was a certain charm about the place because of the quiet. To be surrounded by so much peacefulness was comforting, particularly in the late spring when gentle breezes carried the fragrance of the freshly mowed lawn, and the occasional butterfly, past groups of mourners interring the dead.

"These winters are real crackers, though" she said, as she continued to march along in the snow. "I've heard that sometimes even a backhoe has a heck of a time digging a grave in this frozen dirt!"

The Jungs had moved to the cemetery three years previously, the relocation allowing Jon to step away from the day to day operation of the large scale mortuary practice where he was employed. A doctor had diagnosed Jon with a minor heart condition, at least that's what he had told Ellen. Considering the stressful nature of his job, he thought that getting out of the city would be the wisest step that they could take.

Ellen June, for her part, considered the move as a chance to provide a healthier living environment for Richie. With Ellen and Jon both approaching their middle forties, they saw their coming to a smaller community as the most conducive way to help Richie avoid the typical pitfalls and negative persuasions that would confront him along the way to adulthood.

Ellen gathered the fabric of her coat a little tighter around her body in an effort to stay warm. She was nearing home and was looking forward to the luxury of its heated interior when she came upon a ghastly sight.

On the side of the lone house that existed between the outskirts of town and the memorial park, a mere hundred yards from the cemetery's rot iron gates, she saw the harshness and total indifference that a cold night was capable of producing. A black cat, with arched back, stood silent, frozen, and extremely dead against the house's exterior wall. Its mouth, still open from the last angry hiss offered in futility against the cold, portrayed the anguish of the animal in its final realization that, on this night, at least, with all the cruelty of its indiscriminate brutality, even nine lives would not be enough to allow it to survive.

It was a scene of extreme pathos, and yet, Ellen June's thoughts immediately turned to Mr. Blum, the high school science teacher whom, she believed, would like to have the unfortunate animal as a specimen to be used for dissection by his sophomore biology class.

Ellen June was extremely fond of Mr. Blum. For some reason she had always found herself attracted to short men, perhaps because, even in her day, she was a tall woman, standing at 6 foot 1. Her husband, Jon, was also short, but not nearly as short as the science teacher. Mr. Blum, too, tended towards the rotund, really not unattractive for an obese person, merely fat enough to give him the look of a slightly overgrown cherub.

In her skewed logic, she frequently envisioned Mr. Blum, a chubby little man with short pudgy fingers, as making a good piano player. "Sure," her husband once said when she told him of her thoughts, "if he happened to be sitting before a baby grand in a whorehouse! Other than that, he'd never make it at Carnegie Hall!"

Trudging onward, approaching the cemetery gates, Ellen June could easily make out the gleam of their front porch light, almost glistening in the air of the cold winter night. She quickened her pace in her desire to reach the warmth and comfort of her home. Still, she was troubled over not being able to locate her offspring, and, with foreboding, felt that bad news might be awaiting her upon arrival.

Passing through the open cemetery gates, Ellen June thought it odd that, at this late hour of the night, they had not yet been closed. With heart pounding in concern over her son, wildly imagining the worst possible reason why the gates had not been shut, Ellen quickly covered the thirty yards of the entrance drive, bringing her to the ring road that meandered around the perimeter of the cemetery.

Without bothering to walk the short distance to the driveway that was found on the right side of the house, Ellen June simply marshaled her way across the snow covered lawn that led up to the porch. Climbing its short set of steps, she went to the front door, which was rarely ever locked, took hold of the door knob and opened the door.

Stepping inside and then shutting the door, Ellen remained still for a moment, closing her eyes to better enjoy the warmth of the house. Slowly she removed the scarf from her head, and unbuttoned her coat. Finally, opening her eyes, she looked around the softly lit living room expecting to see Jon, parked in his favorite easy chair, watching the Monday night football game. But even though the TV was on, he wasn't there.

"Jon?" Ellen June called out, hoping to hear a response. But there was no answer.   "Well," she said with wrinkled brow, "perhaps he's in the bathroom?" Puzzled, and still wondering where he might be, she began walking down the adjacent hallway. His absence seemed strange, because Jon, with a fairly healthy set of kidneys, rarely left his chair when the game was being televised. Even during the station breaks he wouldn't leave, because he didn't want to miss the opportunity to see, as Ellen called them, "The scantily clad bimbos parading about on the boob tube hawking beer!"

As Ellen June approached the bathroom, she could see that the door was open, but the light was off.

"Jon?" Ellen said as she came to the door. She reached in for the light switch, found it, and turned it on, but Jon wasn't there.

Ellen June retraced her steps down the hallway and walked back into the living room. Crossing it, she went to the entrance of the kitchen and froze in her tracks at the doorway, for in the middle of the room there was a body covered by a sheet, lying on the kitchen table.

"Gee, I sure wish Jon wouldn't bring his work into the house," Ellen quietly said to herself. Taking a couple of steps closer, wondering why she had a body in her kitchen, she was suddenly struck by a sickening thought: *Maybe this was Richie!* Now fretting, Ellen's mind became filled with a fearful onslaught of unthinkable images: *Maybe he was killed somewhere – maybe it was a horrible death – and Jon went after him – and now Richie is lying there under that sheet!* Momentarily immobilized by fear, it took every ounce of nerve that Ellen June could summons to make her move closer. Surely, she finally and courageously reasoned, there was only one way to discover the truth.

Ellen hesitantly walked over to the table. Stopping next to the shrouded figure, she, with trembling hand, gently reached out to take hold of the sheet. Just as Ellen June was about to pull it back to reveal the identity of the deceased, she was startled by a familiar voice coming from behind her.

"It's an Indian from out on the reservation."

"Darn, Jon!" Ellen gasped, quickly turning to face her husband. "You scared the bejeebers out of me!"

"Sorry," he said with a smile. "I just wanted to see how high you could jump."

"Well, I hate when you do that!" Ellen said. Still miffed, she additionally inquired, "And what's the body of an Indian doing in my kitchen, anyway?"

"The damn fool got stinking drunk and fell into a millpond and drowned. He was like a block of ice! I brought him in here to thaw out so I can embalm him." Then Jon added, "Who did you think you'd find under there, for Pete's sake?"

"Your son!" Ellen replied. "Have you heard from him?"

"Yeah, he called about a half hour ago from the horizontal recreation area."

"You mean, Susan's house?"

5

"Yep, same place."

"Do you have to refer to it by that name? Richie's an impressionable young boy and I don't want him to get the idea that women are only good for one thing."

"And that would be?" Jon asked, point blank. "I'm still hoping to make that discovery."

"You know full well what I'm talking about, Jon!"

"He's just a healthy young boy with a curiosity – that's all," Jon asserted. "He's normal."

Having now gone full tilt into her maternal protective mode Ellen said, "Richie needs to know that what goes on over at Susan's house with her mother certainly is *not normal* fair! He has to realize that there's more to a woman than just her body, and looking at the men's magazine you have in the bathroom won't help him learn that, either."

Jon stood gazing up at the ceiling in a moment of fond recollection, a dubious smile on his face. "A great issue," he finally said, dreamily, "June of 1964 – the Girls of Texas–a very spectacular pictorial!"

"Well, we don't need it in our house – it's embarrassing to have our guests go into the bathroom and be confronted by that magazine!"

"The men don't seem to mind," Jon said.

"But the women do, so take it out to the back office!"

"Who's the stiff?" A voice suddenly asked from the doorway.

Upon hearing the voice Ellen said, "Richie!" She turned to face her son, and then rushed over to give him a hug. "I was worried sick about you!"

"I was over at Susan's, studying for a test," Richie said.

"Well, I don't like you going over there. Her mother is a shameless woman of easy virtue – I don't want you to be around her."

"She's harmless," Richie responded.

"She's a tramp," Ellen June harped, "and I don't want you over at her house!"

"Meow!" Jon blurted out. "It's only a cat house!"

"You're not helping, Jon," Ellen directed towards her husband. She then looked at her son and said, "Why don't you bring Susan over here to study?"

"This place creeps her out, Mom."

"If she only comes into the house, she'd be fine."

"She thinks we have bodies lying all over the place," Richie said. Pointing to the kitchen table he furthered, "And again, if you don't mind, who's the stiff?"

"It's an Indian from the reservation," Ellen said. She looked over at Jon and glared at him, adding, "Your father brought him into the kitchen to warm him up a bit."

"Fell into the millpond and froze solid," Jon quickly interjected. "Couldn't get a tube into him for embalming."

Jon actually didn't do much embalming on the premises anymore. He only infrequently worked on indigent persons – those that couldn't afford the services of the funeral establishments in town. For this, Jon received only a modest fee from the county.

"No more, Jon!" Ellen said. "From now on you keep your work out back. No wonder that poor girl is afraid to come over here!"

Jon walked over to the table and threw back the part of the sheet that covered the head of deceased. The profile of the man's face could have easily served as a model for the "Indian Head" nickel. Thanks to the room's heat, the occasional drop of water, released from the man's clothes as in the spring melt of a winter's snow, was now falling onto the kitchen floor. Gently slapping the fellow a couple of times on the cheek and poking him in the ribcage, Jon made his determination.

"He's thawed enough."

Bringing his face close to the Indian's head, Jon spoke directly to the departed. "Come on, Chief, let's go get you ready for the big powwow in the sky!"

Straightening up, he turned to Richie.

"Why don't you help your old man take our guest out back?"

"Sure thing, Dad!"

"Let's put him on the gurney," Jon said, pushing it up against the kitchen table where the dead man rested in eternal repose. "You take his feet, and I'll get him by the shoulders."

Richie and Jon moved to opposite ends of the body. "Goodnight, Chief," Jon quietly said as he gave the man an affectionate pat on the cheek. He then took the sheet and flipped it back over the man's head.

"You two be careful!" Ellen June said from across the room. "I don't want you to get hurt."

"Alright, Richie. Are you ready?"

The boy nodded his head.

"Okay! Now!" Jon directed.

With some effort, the son and the father were able to lift the dead man slightly and then slide him onto the gurney.

"Make sure you strap him in real good. I don't want him to fall off and sue us!"

"He's dead, Dad!" Richie told his father.

"I know," Jon returned, "but I don't want to take any chances!"

An elderly gentleman, in his late seventies, suddenly appeared at the kitchen door.

"Did I get a phone call from Agent X 100?" He asked.

"Dad," Ellen softly said to the aged man, "did we wake you up?"

The man was actually Jon's father, but Ellen June fondly thought of him as her own."

"I wasn't asleep. I was working on a very important assignment. I'm waiting for Agent X 100 to call with the new code so I can decipher the latest message from the department. We don't want those Russkies finding out about our secrets! In government intelligence, we take our work very seriously!"

"Now, Dad," Ellen June said sweetly, "you know you've never worked for the government." She looked at Jon and asked, "Did he take his medication today?"

"I don't know," Jon answered, "why don't you ask him?"

Ellen merely frowned at her husband.

Jon turned to his father and asked, "Dad, did you take your sugar pill already?"

"I'll have to look at my check off sheet, won't I?" The old man surly responded.

Ellen June walked over to the sink, took a glass and drew some tap water. She went over to the elderly man and handed it to him. "Here, Dad. Why don't you take this to your room and see if you need another pill. They're on the night stand next to your bed."

Jon's father took the glass and walked out of the kitchen, muttering to himself. "Agent X 100 has to contact me soon! It's very important. I have to get the information about our first shipment!"

When the elder Jung was finally out of the room, Ellen June spoke up.

"You know your dad needs that medication to help him control his fantasies, Jon."

"What's wrong with him having a few fantasies?" Jon asked. He turned to Richie and winked. "At his age, that all he's got left!"

Richie smiled, gently.

"For crying out loud, Jon! Your dad has worked in the funeral business all his life!"

"Are you sure about that?" Jon inquired with a wry smile.

"Honestly!" Ellen responded. "We can't encourage these illusions about his having worked for a spy agency of the government."

"They're innocuous, really," Jon replied.

"Yes, but they get in the way of his coping with reality."

"So?"

"You're hopeless!" Ellen said in frustration.

Jon only smiled.

Turning back to the task at hand, Jon took hold of his end of the gurney and said to Richie, "Come on, Son, let's take the Chief out to the teepee in the back so we can put on his war paint."

"OK Kemosabe," Richie said, using his Indian voice imitation, "you push 'em, me pull 'em!"

Jon, likewise, uttered, "Ugh!"

Two

While Jon was preparing the deceased for burial, Richie watched the process, helping where he could. He hadn't yet decided if he was going to make his living in the family business. Handling dead bodies wasn't particularly bothersome to him. Only when the deceased were children did he have a problem.

When they first moved into their home, Richie spent a lot of time walking through the cemetery, looking at the graves. The place was peaceful – quiet. He found an aloneness here that appealed to his sense of loss, having said goodbye to his friends when his family came to this area. As Richie read the grave markers, he'd glance at the birth and death dates, roughly calculate the age of the person, and try to imagine the cause of death.

The cemetery was ample for a town of its size – large enough, in fact, that Richie couldn't study all of the grave sites in a matter of just a few hours. His initial inspection actually came on the very day they had arrived from the city. Subsequently, over the course of the next few months, his explorations quietly continued as he habitually wandered the narrow rows of analogous grave markers on a weekly basis.

Two of the headstones, situated on plots right next to each other, did, however, capture his immediate attention on that first day of exploration. They were the graves of two twelve year old girls. Each had been born in the same year as he, and both had died on the very same day a few years prior to his visit to the graves. Richie felt an affinity for the two, simply because the girls, had they lived, would now be about his own age.

Having met neither, he nevertheless endeavored to imagine, in a general sense, how they would now appear - with smiling faces, always laughing – carefree young ladies full of life. In a stroke of irony, by a mere chance of pure happenstance, death had taken all of that from the two. Briefly, he mourned for the future that they had lost – lives unfulfilled from the challenges they may have faced, cruelly deprived even of the happiness of intangible, simple pleasures – no prom dates, nor careers, no love, nor marriage, or children. Their deaths made no sense to him.

Richie surmised that the two had been friends and had come to death from the same tragic event. Later, he asked his father if he knew what had happened to them, and if their deaths were related. Jon prided himself on knowing the circumstances behind the deaths of many of those that were already interred before he and his family had moved onto the grounds, these young girls included. His answer verified his son's suspicions – the girls had drowned in a nearby lake while coming to the aid of a frightened dog. The animal was pulled into a passing boat and survived.

Richie didn't usually grieve while inspecting the grave markers, however. That, he felt, was a private matter for the attending mourners at the grave site. Though quiet and respectful while slowly strolling past a burial service in progress, he was mostly immune to the emotions of bereavement, feeling almost privileged, instead, to be privy to the goings on soon to take place behind the scene.

These were what could be called the nuts and bolts of a cemetery burial to which people, in general, didn't give much thought. There was prep work that went on before the service: the opening of the grave (usually with a backhoe); the insertion of a concrete liner into which the casket would be lowered; the placement of artificial turf on each side of the grave opening; and the setting up of the catafalque assembly (Jon's name for what was known in the trade as a "casket lowering device" – he thought his designation was more classy) that would cradle the coffin on heavy cloth straps over the open grave.

Afterwards, preferably when the mourners had already departed, the casket would be lowered into the grave; the catafalque was removed; the phony green grass rolled back from the edge and taken away; a series of concrete slabs were then set in place to seal the underlying pre-cast liner; dirt would be dropped by the backhoe into the open grave, completely filling it; and finally, pieces of cut sod were laid on top of the grave.

Mundane jobs to be sure, not requiring Rhodes' scholars by any stretch of the imagination to accomplish; these tasks were left to an unsophisticated gang of cemetery workers from the lower end of the skills spectrum to carry out. Attentive and courteous while the boss was around, the group became lackadaisical and much too casual when he departed. Richie saw this firsthand one day, and later considered this to be an important introduction to the beginning of his informal education on what made people tick. He had gone to a grave site seeking counsel from his father on women. Jon was making his way around the grave, lifting each corner of the casket lowering device and removing the green artificial lawn from beneath its legs.

"I'm the last person you should be coming to for advice about them," Jon said with a grunt as he picked up one corner of the catafalque. "I know nothing about women!"

"But you married Mom!"

Jon gave out a little laugh, and then said, "Yeah?"

"Well?"

Straining to lift another corner of the casket lowing device with the coffin still in place, Jon said, "I've seen this woman around town, but I didn't think she was this heavy!" Going to the last corner and removing the final piece of artificial turf, Jon finally said, "Look, your mom was pretty straight forward — she knew what she wanted out of life — she was the first female embalmer in the state, for crying out loud! Most women are insecure — they aren't sure about anything, not even themselves. But your mom wasn't like that."

"Why do you think she was different?" Richie inquired.

"Beats me," Jon answered. "Women are a riddle wrapped in a mystery inside an enigma, as far as I'm concerned. They always have been and always will be!"

"But," Richie said, "you can't live with them and you can't live without them, right?"

"You can't live with them and you can't live with them!" Jon responded.

"What?"

"You have your version, I have mine."

"Couldn't be more vague, could you?" Richie offered in frustration.

Jon smiled and said, "You'll learn with time and experience."

"Isn't there an easier way?"

"Nope."

"That's reassuring."

"Well," Jon said with a smile, "I'm done here. Time for lunch. Are you coming?"

"No, Dad. I just had breakfast."

"Oh, I forgot — it's part of the teenage sleep in late routine — isn't it?"

"Yeah, got to do my part to uphold our reputation, you know."

"Your mom's fixing some of her famous pickled watermelon rind. I'll save a piece for you."

"That's all right — you can have my share."

"You don't know what you're missing!"

"Yes, Dad, I do."

"Well, I'm off," Jon said. As he walked over to his pickup truck he looked up at the sky and added, "Looks like rain later today."

Richie waved to his dad and watched as he drove away. He then looked over at one of the cemetery workers who was now, since Jon had departed, leaning against his shovel in a relaxed pose, a shit eating grin on his face.

"I'm surprised he didn't say anything about clabbered milk," the worker said.

"He's told you that story, too?" Richie inquired.

"Yeah, we know all about how your dad worked on a farm when he was a kid – and how the rain storms and thunder scared them cows and soured the milk." The man was laughing when he said, "I bet it made their eyes get as big as their a-holes!" He then asked Richie, "How young was you when you heard it for the first time?"

"I don't know – maybe eight or nine."

"Heard it often, too?"

Richie responded, "Every time there was a storm, every time the milk went bad, every time a freaking cow was heard nervously mooing in the distance!"

The man laughed again as one of the other workers called his name.

"Hey, Lou? Can we lower the coffin now?"

Lou was the foreman of the group, even though it was an informal designation.

"Yeah, I guess we're ready." Then, with authority in his voice gained from years of experience on the job he said, "Go ahead – lower away!"

As the casket was being lowered, two of the foreman's co-workers from the three man crew took hold of the straps from the casket lowering device and began guiding the coffin into the pre-cast liner.

"Careful!" Lou warned. "That's a ten thousand dollar casket. We don't want to bang it up *too* much!"

The two workers gently pushed and pulled the straps, allowing only minimal contact between the concrete box and the pricey burial unit.

"Who'd be crazy enough to pay all that money for something you was just going to rot in?" Lou asked to no one in particular.

"Maybe a rich guy with a guilty conscious?" Richie chimed in. He then added, "Had to take care of dear old Mumsie, didn't he?"

With the coffin resting in place, the straps were extracted and the casket lowering device removed.

"Hey, Lenny," the foreman said, "why don't yous get down in the hole and start laying them slabs." Lou looked at Richie and added, "Don't want all that dirt to crush Mumsie, do we?"

As commanded, Lenny, using the two edges of the grave for support, gingerly began lowering himself into the middle of the hole, making sure to carefully place his shoes on the sides of the concrete liner, and not the casket.

"Okay, Pete," he said, "start handing me the slabs."

Taking hold of one of the concrete forms with both hands, Lenny leaned over and placed the roughly two feet, by one foot, by one inch piece on the top of the pre-cast liner box at the very end of the grave.

"All right, Slowpoke, give me another."

Lenny was handed a second slab and repeated the process.

"All right, another!" But Pete was slow in delivering a third slab as well, so Lenny chastised him with, "Come on, will ya! I don't have all day!"

With three slabs laid down, Lenny stepped onto the newly formed top for the per-cast liner and turned around.

"All right, another," he commanded, snapping his fingers for emphasis. He then took hold of the slab and set it in place.

"I knew a rich kid once, when me and a bunch of friends was young," Lou suddenly said out of the blue.

Richie merely raised his eyebrows in surprise when hearing the remark – not because he didn't believe that the foreman could have known someone relatively well-off, but instead, because he was doubtful that that level of affluence had actually existed in the town.

"He was a real smart kid, and we was pretty dumb," Lou freely admitted. "We'd trade him dimes for nickels – we thought nickels was worth more because they was bigger. He's a lawyer now, and we're burying stiffs in a bone yard!"

"Maybe that's his mom?" Richie quipped, pointing to the grave.

"Maybe," Lou said, his shit eating grin spreading across his face.

Lenny, having put the last slab into position on top of the pre-cast liner, stomped across the slabs from end to end to make sure they stayed in place.

"Hey Numb Nuts," Lenny directed to Pete, "come help get me out!"

Pete went over to the grave and handed the spade end of a shovel to Lenny. Taking the tool, turning it so the back side of the shovel was facing him, Lenny placed the handle against the dirt wall at the end of the grave and then put the tip of the blade between the first two slabs. Stepping gingerly onto the space with his left foot while grabbing the handle with his left hand, Lenny extended his right arm so that Pete could take his hand and help him out of the grave.

"Hey, Lou," Lenny said when reaching topside, "should I go get the backhoe?"

"Gees!" Lou answered. "Have a little respect for the dead! Put a few shovels of dirt in first – and gently, I tell ya! Then we'll use the tractor."

Richie, seeing that the work was almost complete said, "Well, I guess I'll get going."

"Don't yous want to stick around and help, kid," the foreman asked.

"No, I think I'll go have lunch."

"I thought yous said you just had breakfast?"

"Yeah, I did," Richie responded, "but that was thirty minutes ago!"

Three

Living in a house situated on a cemetery wasn't as unnerving as most people might think. It *was* quiet there, but then, that was one of its charms.

Still, Richie didn't like to draw any undue attention to the fact that his family's residence was located within the boundaries of the local marble orchard. He didn't even like to admit to the existence of any association with the handling of dead bodies, or their interment.

If asked what his father did for a living, Richie would frequently respond with a casual, offhand remark: "He's kind of in real estate," he'd say with a smile approaching a smirk, "he buys land by the acre, and sells it by the inch."

With the occasional connotation of the macabre aside, there was truly nothing darkly foreboding about the nature of the family business. There was, however, unbeknownst to Richie, something nebulously sinister that was about to be put into place.

On the edge of town, on the main thoroughfare that transited the burgh, there was a large, innocuous looking white building. Viewed from the street, the right-hand portion was dedicated to office space; the larger section on the left was clearly designed for manufacturing and warehousing. For years the facility had been utilized for the production of weed killer, with little or no regard for the waste products that had been dumped into the nearby creek, making the firm a gross polluter.

Although it was the last building seen while leaving the town, or the first in view upon entering, the locals gave little notice to the activities associated with the site. It had, however, gained some notoriety of late when a teenage girl ignored the hard ninety degree right turn the road made in front of the building coming into town, accelerated her car deliberately to drive straight into the building, killing her instantly upon impact.

Sadly, some misguided local high school youths (it was assumed) took it upon themselves to paint an obscenely large bull's-eye at the very point where the car had crashed into the building, ending the girl's life. Thankfully, the city fathers were able to arrange to have the unsightly target spot painted over within a matter of months.

Oddly, the building had escaped notice as a busy hub for shipping and receiving (the loading dock was located on the left-hand side of the building, visible only to those that might find themselves, for whatever reason, on the dead end street that fronted that segment of the facility): the arrival and departure of transports were usually scheduled, to be less intrusive, under the cloak of darkness, and then, rather late in night.

Because the business of what occurred on those premises was vague and primarily hidden, either by accident or by design (the windows on the street side being largely opaque, with inner light barely visible from the outside), it never became apparent to the local residents just when the firm operating the weed killer plant decided to pack up its operation and close its doors.

The name of the product, "Weed-B-Gone", had been painted on the front of the building near its roof line up until a year or so before Richie and his family had moved to the town. With the removal of that name, purposely hidden beneath a coat of dirty white paint that barely matched the fading pallid tone of the rest of the nondescript façade of the structure, everyone thought that the site was derelict and no longer in use. For the moment, that was the case. But soon, that would change.

Four

On a lazy spring afternoon, Jon and Richie were returning to the cemetery in the company hearse. Having had routine maintenance performed on the vehicle, they were traveling at a respectable rate of speed through town. Richie, on this day, avoided his usual youthful prank of reclining in the back of the hearse, rising up while at a stop sign to wave at the unsuspecting driver in the following car. Actually, the idea had actually been Jon's, who always got a chuckle out of seeing the reaction that invariably occurred.

Riding "shotgun" for his dad in the right front seat, Richie was keeping a keen eye peeled for a woman that they would frequently see out walking while they were driving in town.

"There she is, Dad!" Richie said when he spotted the woman. Giving directions, pointing, he said, "She's over there on the right!"

Jon glanced in her direction, smiled slightly, but said nothing.

"You have to do it, Dad! She's right there!" Richie said, trying to coax his father into his act.

Jon said, "Well . . ." He looked over at Richie and gave him a quick little grin. Clearing his throat, Jon began speaking - narrating, in a flat voice, everything that the woman, thirty something and rather plain looking, was doing – adding subtle, inferred comments about her thoughts.

"She decided to wear a long sleeved sweater, even though the day was rather warm, choosing perspiration over the possibility of skin cancer. Her small purse, suspended from a strap around her neck, was nestled safe and secure under her armpit, next to her barely perceivable bosom. Its contents? A hanky and a pack of cigarettes – *Camels*, not Virginia Slims. She was no wuss!

"Having long since given up on finding the man of her dreams, she, nonetheless, slowed down considerably in front of the construction site of the town's new fire station, hoping to garner some attention from the guys on the job. Savoring the occasional wolf-whistle, she still found offense at being rated as only a "2" on their girl watching scale of "0" to "10". 'I could be at least an "8",' she'd say, 'if I only had a six pack of beer!'"

Richie smiled over his dad's performance, and chuckled at his humor. A while back, Jon had actually considered committing the narrative about the woman to writing for publication.

"What were you going to call your story, again?" Richie asked.

"Walking Without Purpose," Jon said, 'but I don't think I could come up with enough material to sustain a complete book."

"But you should write it, Dad. It's funny!"

17

"Well, maybe I could incorporate it into another story – you know, the novel I've always intended to write about the midgets that abandon the circus in a small town and open a funeral home that caters to their own kind in hopes of a better life."

"Little people," Richie said.

"Excuse me?"

"I believe they like to be called 'little people'," Richie reiterated.

"A midget is a midget," Jon returned.

"Unless they're a dwarf, and then they still prefer the term, 'little people'."

"Whatever," Jon said, slightly flustered, "anyway," he quickly added, "I thought I'd call the book, Three Feet Under/When You Come Up Short."

"I'm sure you'd win the Pulitzer for that one."

"Money in the bank!" Jon exclaimed with a twinkle in his eye.

Looking into the side mirror of the hearse, Richie could still see the woman making her way up the street. He turned to Jon and said, "Mom saw her out walking once and thought the woman looked pregnant – she had a little bump for her tummy, but then, it went away."

"I wonder who would . . ." Jon offered without finishing the thought. "She's kind of a strange duck," he then said, "I mean, she does strike me as the sort of person who causes the lights to dim whenever she walks into a room. Perhaps, as humorist James Thurber had observed, she might just be one of those people that causes things to go 'bump' in the middle of the night? Still, I feel sorry for the woman – she's as plain as day. Who do you think might find her attractive?"

"For some guys, all the woman needs is a pulse," Richie answered.

"And for some of the sickos in our business, sometimes they don't even need that!"

Jon glanced down at the fuel gauge. "I better stop at a gas station and gas up the hog. Wanna hop in the back so you can wave to some folks on the way home?"

"Sure. Why not? I'm in the mood for some laughs!"

Five

Ellen was standing at the kitchen counter preparing the ingredients to marinate the Sauerbraten for the evening meal. It was a tedious task, but it was Jon's favorite meal and she would do anything for him, simply because she loved him so much. She did balk, however, at making Spatzle (German noodles), choosing instead to Americanize the dish by substituting mashed potatoes.

Jon's father came gingerly into the kitchen, constantly peering over his shoulder. Moving spryly as possible for a gentleman of 78, not quite pulling off his attempt at casual stealth, Samuel Jung sidled up to Ellen June's right side.

"Any word from Agent X 100 yet?" He said in a whisper.

"Oh! Dad! You startled me!" Ellen said as she was putting a knife to a carrot.

"We *all* have to be alert," Jon' father warned, still talking in a low voice. He then added, "Well?"

"Dad," Ellen June replied, "why are you whispering?"

"The room might be bugged!" The old man said, still speaking softly.

"I think you're the only thing bugged around here, Dad," Ellen said. "There is no Agent X 100. You don't work for the government!"

"Are you sure?" Samuel said, now in a regular voice, but in a way that could show either confusion or affirmation upon hearing, depending on the listener's frame of mind.

"Dad," Ellen June said sweetly, "we bury dead people here."

"Exactly!"

"You see? That has nothing to do with a government intelligence agency."

"We bury dead people here!" Jon's father said, repeating and emphasizing Ellen June's words in a very positive manner, but once again, in a whisper.

"Yes, we do," Ellen reaffirmed.

"Okay," the old man softly said, "but let me know when Agent X 100 calls. I *need* that new code!"

"Oh, good grief," Ellen June said in frustration under her breath.

"Can I have a cookie, now?" Jon's father asked with obvious pleasure.

Six

"I think the site's perfect," Richie heard his dad say on the phone while passing by his father's office one afternoon. He pressed his ear against the closed door to better hear his father as he started to wrap up the conversation. "You can get the place for a song," his dad said. "It's been abandoned for a couple of years now – the receiving area can't even be seen from the street – it's a good setup."

Richie couldn't imagine what his father was talking about, but when he heard his dad say that they could start up operations and the place would still look deserted, one building in town immediately came to Richie's mind – the old Weed-B-Gone plant.

"I'll do some snooping around and get a line on the place," his dad said. He then asked, "Do we have a cover story in the pipe line just in case?"

Jon listened as the caller explained what was waiting in the wings if someone happened to get curious. "Sounds good," he finally said. "I'll get back to you in a couple of days."

Puzzled over this discourse, and what may have just been inadvertently revealed, Richie pulled his ear away from the door, momentarily lost in silent thought. Slowly, he brought his arm up from his side, and making a fist, knocked on the door. Without waiting for an invitation from his father to enter, Richie opened the door and stepped into the room.

"I couldn't help hearing you on the phone when I was passing by," Richie said to his father. "What was that call all about?"

With an out of place smile of a child who had just been caught with his hand in the cookie jar, Jon slowly pushed his chair back from his desk, stood up, and walked over to his son. Cautiously moving behind the boy, Jon gently closed the door, placed his arm across Richie's shoulders, and led him over to the desk. The father turned to stand face to face with his son. He instinctively gazed over his shoulders, then looked at the boy and winked.

"Don't tell your mother," Jon said, "but I think I may have come across a great way to scare up some extra money!"

"No punning around, Dad," Richie said.

""I'm not," Jon replied, smiling slightly. "This might turn out to be a sweet deal."

"Is it legal?"

"Well, the mob's not involved, if that's what you're thinking."

"Okay," Richie said, "but is it ethical?"

"I don't think ethics come into play here."

"So, what is it?" Richie inquired.

"I can't tell you," Jon told him. "All I can say is that it's contract work."

"All right, if it's not organized crime, who else could it be? Can you tell me that?"

Jon remained silent.

Richie looked at this father for a moment and then calmly asked, "What are you hiding, Dad?"

The father still said nothing.

The boy thought for a moment and then smiled. "Wait a minute," he finally said, "do you mean to tell me that you're immersed in some kind of clandestine government operation? That's really cool!"

"I never said that," Jon quickly responded.

"Come on, Dad. You can tell me. I won't say anything."

Jon, thinking for a moment, then said, "Maybe someday."

Richie only said, "Hmm." He then added, "So, what's it going to cost you?"

"Cost me?" Jon said in a bewildered reply.

"You can't do this sort of business with the government without paying some kind of price. They'll have a foothold on you – what is it?"

"I can tell you nothing," was all Jon would willingly say.

Richie stared at his father for a moment in silence. Then, beginning to smile, he turned slightly from his father and raised his arm. With his hand painting a word picture, Richie said, "All you have to do is give us your first born male child!"

Jon remained silent.

With smile fading, Richie, now with a serious frame of mind, addressed his dad. "Wait a minute," he quietly said, "you're not really thinking about enlisting me in some program of indentured servitude with the government, are you?"

Calmly, without rushing, Jon asked, "What are your plans for the future, Son?"

Richie, not quite knowing how to reply, said, "Well, I thought I'd finish high school first, and then take over Hugh Hefner's empire."

"Really?" Jon gleefully asked.

"No!" Richie shot back. "I don't know what I want to do - not yet!"

Unhurriedly, again calmly, Jon asked, "Ever thought about a career in government?"

"What as? A bean counting overworked pencil pusher? No thanks!"

"Nothing as mundane as that," Jon replied. "How about working in government intelligence?"

"Isn't that an oxymoron?"

Jon, with a wry smile, said, "Just think about it, Son. Okay?"

Seven

"I'd wait a while before you go into the bathroom," Jon said as he walked into the kitchen. "Whew! It must have been that Sauerbraten and potatoes we had last night."

"Did you clean up after yourself and take that girlie magazine out of there?" Ellen June asked.

"Yes, yes, it's spotless – as always," Jon replied.

Richie was at the kitchen table, eating a bowl of cereal. He looked up at his dad, a confused expression on his face.

In response, Jon said, "Your mother is under the distinct impression that The Queen of England is going to drop in one day, wanting to use our bathroom – so we *must* keep it tidy!"

"You're kidding, right?" Richie remarked. "Do you know the odds against that ever happening?"

"Astronomical," Jon answered.

"Mock me if you must," Ellen said, "but I can feel it in my bones. One day, she's going to be here!"

Jon looked at his son with raised eyebrows and said, "God save The Queen!"

"I wonder who's assigned to wipe her . . . ." Richie pondered. "Oh, never mind," he finally concluded.

"Richie!" Ellen June uttered.

Then Jon added his measured opinion. "You know, nothing would strip away the crown, metaphorically, faster than envisioning The Queen sitting upon the throne, and I don't mean the Royal one, either."

"Jon!" Ellen directed towards her husband, clearly showing her displeasure.

"Would you call that a Royal Flush?" Richie queried.

"You two are just terrible!" Ellen June said. "I'm not going to stay and listen to any more of this!" With that, she turned and began walking out of the kitchen.

"Fragrance wise," Richie added to the mix, "I wonder how the Royal Turd compares to a specimen delivered up by one of us common folk?"

"Ooh!" Ellen responded in the distance, obviously in disgust.

"Richer," Jon then offered, with a smile. "Decidedly richer!"

22

Eight

Looking into the bathroom mirror, Richie was trying to decide if he should go downtown and get a haircut. It was the 1960s and attitudes were changing about styles in clothing and in the length of men's hair. He wasn't quite sure how he wanted to wear his hair, but Richie thought it might look better if it was a little longer. He was certain, however, that his dad would probably rib him about the haircut, but in reality, Jon couldn't care less about the length of his son's hair, as long as it appeared to be neat.

The problem, Richie surmised, would be with the guy cutting his hair. "Vic the Barber", as he was universally known, was referred to in the same affectionate tone and with the identical reverence as one might possess when calling to mind the likes of "Attila the Hun" or "Genghis Khan". Basically, as Richie figured, they all had their origins in the same neighborhood – that was so say, nomadic, crude, and demonic (in Vic's case, at least, in a rascally way).

The barber had been in the U.S. Army, of sorts, during the Second World War. While in training camp, Vic was either AWOL, or in the brig serving time for being AWOL. He could handle a rifle all right, and obviously was a fast runner, since he was always able to give the MPs the slip – but Vic had absolutely no respect for authority, military or otherwise. When the army actually did manage to successfully ship him out to the Pacific, Vic was placed in handcuffs and kept locked up until the troop transport was at least ten miles off the coast, hoping to prevent him from grabbing a life preserver and jumping ship, as he did in San Francisco Bay the first time it was attempted to send him overseas.

It was a gutsy move on Vic's part, because he couldn't swim – and he almost got away with it, too – but unfortunately, he wasn't picked up, as he had hoped, by one of the numerous party boats cruising on the Bay. The United States Coast Guard hauled him out of the water, instead. He let it be known, after the war, that he preferred the brig of the coast guard much more than that of the army – better chow, he claimed.

Vic eventually made it to the Pacific Theater, but his time on the front line was rather brief. At dusk on the first day of battle in the jungle, his platoon dug in and he spent the night with a buddy in a foxhole, nervously waiting for the dawn. In the morning, while the two soldiers were congratulating each other for having survived the terrors of war in the darkness, a sniper's bullet suddenly whizzed over the top of Vic's helmet and smashed into the forehead of his foxhole partner. Well, that pushed Vic over the edge.

He clambered out of the foxhole and started running. Vic didn't remember anything about his escape – how far he had run, or how he had managed to land in the mental ward of an army hospital sometime later. But after whatever cerebral process had enabled him to elude the fearful situation, the mental fog that had enveloped his brain would eventually be dispelled and he would awaken, only to find himself handcuffed to a military prison hospital bed. His plan had always been to pull off some kind of "Section Eight" scam to win his release from the service, but this had turned out much better than he had hoped. Vic didn't have to pretend to be crazy to get what he wanted. The doctors had determined that, because of his traumatic experience in the foxhole, Vic actually was nuts – clearly unfit for duty – and that proved to be his "million dollar" ticket home!

After the excitement of being shot at during the war, Vic was at a loss as to what he wanted to do in civilian life to make a living for himself so that he could support his wife and child. Then he hit upon an idea of how he could recreate the camaraderie of his army days – he'd open a barbershop! It would be the archetypical model of the once and future man cave – a bastion of male bonding where females dare not enter – nay, neither would they even attempt to pass the boundaries of the premises and befoul the sanctuary of the brotherhood, besmirching the birthright of every man to find peace in a hallowed place, free from the unwanted interference of the womenfolk. No, the nag would definitely not be welcomed!

And what of the atmosphere therein? Smoking? To be sure – and ashtrays would be allowed to overflow! Men's magazines? You bet – with hot babes, hot cars, and firearms galore! Unrestrained scratching, swearing, and wolf-whistling at shapely young things that passed by the barbershop door would be the norm. A guy couldn't ask for more!

Richie found his time in the barbershop to be rather amusing. The machismo exhibited in the place was so exaggerated that he felt this surely had to be the last vestige of the primal man in the changing world. Richie wasn't certain, either, if "Vic the Barber" could survive the transition toward the new age of hair styling – the trend could clearly be seen poised on the horizon.

The barber specialized in the "flat top", the "butch", and the "razor cut". Any expressed desire of a man to wear his hair in a longer style contrary to the accepted norm was suspect – tantamount to being un-American, in fact. When Richie walked by the front of the shop and saw a poster of a young man with long hair displayed in the window with the caption, "Beautify America – Get a Haircut!", he knew he had better just ask for a trim. He silently wondered if he'd have the guts to go to a beauty salon in the future whenever he needed a haircut.

When Richie walked into the barbershop, Vic was already finishing up a customer in the chair. Two other guys were queued in the seats that lined the wall. From the informal pecking order established and adhered to from long ago, an adult male was next in line, while a frightened little boy nervously sat, fidgeting in a chair, waiting for his turn in sequence. Richie occupied the seat next to the child. Soon afterwards, two more men walked in, filling up all the spaces in the shop.

In the concluding rite for the haircut that had just been given, Vic removed a clip from an expanse of cloth that was secured around the patron's neck. It caught the hair clippings and kept them from collecting on the customer's shirt and pants. Then Vic gingerly placed his index finger under the thin ribbon of white paper that kept the cloth from chaffing the client's neck and quickly pulled it away from the skin, allowing it to gently fall to the floor. Taking a dry brush that was identical to one that would ordinarily be used to apply the lathered crème for a shave, Vic would ceremoniously whisk away any remaining hair clippings from the patron's neck and shoulders, and then, in a sweeping gesture resembling that of a matador, quickly, but elegantly, remove the cloth from the customer's chest and lap.

Sometimes, too, and it didn't happen with every client, Vic would pull out an electric hand vibrator and massage the customer's shoulders for a minute or two. Richie had seen this done several times before, and the only description he could render to define the expression on the selected client's face was one of complete and utter blissfulness. This was customer service to the hilt.

When the guy from the barber's chair had paid Vic and was walking out the door, the next customer in the queue, the adult male, went over to ascent the barber's throne, so to speak. With that, all the other patrons moved over to the next chair as they waited their turn. Sure as shooting, as soon as the last chair was vacant, another client came into the shop and filled the empty slot.

The fellow now sitting in the barber's chair waiting to receive Vic's attention was bald, or nearly so, with only a fringe of hair sparsely covering the back of the man's head. This, Richie thought, wouldn't take long – but he was wrong. The barber wanted every customer to feel as though they were getting their money's worth. So, Vic followed the same routine with this fellow as with all the others. He placed a fresh ribbon of white paper around the man's neck; took clean crisp linen from a cabinet under the counter and artfully tossed it over the fellow's lap and chest; and then secured the cloth in place around the man's neck with a bright silver clip in such a way to provide just the right amount of tautness in the fabric.

Sure, there was less hair for Vic to cut, but he slowed his pace down a little - repositioning his arms in quick strokes a few more times before cutting – worked the scissors a little more diligently, even making additional cutting motions in the empty air to aid his timing. Vic would chew the fat with the fellow – ask him if he had heard any dirty jokes lately – did everything he could, in fact, to pamper the man, and low and behold, the guy would give Vic a generous tip when he paid for his haircut. Then, saying that he'd see Vic the following week, he'd walk to the door, smiling.

Richie had seen the barber perform the same act on numerous bald men before, but he couldn't understand why they would return so willingly in such a short time when it was obvious that they didn't even need a haircut. The young man overlooked the psychology involved in simply making a person feel good about themselves.

The little boy came next. Vic had a whole special routine set aside for each young boy that came into his shop, and he played it for maximum effect. Before the poor kid even got out of the waiting chair, already visibly shaken, Vic started giving him the sternest of looks. He did that for two reasons. First, to genuinely let the young fellow know who was in charge. Secondly, to cement into place the fear that the child was already experiencing as he went through the ordeal involved in getting his hair cut.

Vic didn't even smile at the boy, but as the youngster made his way to the barber's chair with his eyes cast down, looking at the floor, Vic would flash a quick rascally grin to the rest of the guys in the shop to let them in on the caper.

The small fry wouldn't sit high enough for Vic to be able to cut their hair if they sat in the regular seat of the barber's chair, so a booster seat – a board upholstered with Naugahyde - was employed. Before the lad could step up onto the chair's footrest, Vic would put up his hand and loudly say in a serious voice, "Stay down!" With the boy still looking down, Vic would quickly shoot another naughty grin to the guys.

Going over to the end of the counter that fronted the shop's large mirrors, Vic would reach down in the space between the counter and the shop wall and retrieve the booster seat that had been propped up, endwise, in the corner. Bringing it back to the barber's chair, he'd place the booster seat between the two armrests, pushing it against the back of the chair. Gingerly, even tenderly, Vic would hoist the child up onto the seat but then, continuing with his act, would sternly say, "Hold on!" The boy, thinking perhaps the chair would somehow be magically propelled in excess of 100 mph, would wrap his fingers around the front of the booster seat and grab the thing so tight that his knuckles would turn white.

Standing between the barber chair and the counter, Vic would hold his outstretched arm across the front of the youngster's chest to safeguard the child in a gesture of authentic concern, and at the same time, reach into the cabinet to take out a fresh cloth to place over the top of the boy's clothes. Placing the paper ribbon around the boy's neck and securing the cloth with the silver clip, Vic would then say with a firm voice, "Sit up straight!" When the boy wiggled about in his seat to make himself as tall as he could, Vic, to his audience's delight, would deliver his signature commanding edict. "Sit still, you little shitass, or I'll cut your ear off!"

Well, with that pronouncement, the kid turned as white as a ghost, the guys in the shop chuckled softly so as not to bruise the youngster's ego, and "Vic the Barber" stood, once more, sporting that rascally grin on his face.

From then on, the barber took it easy on the kid. He'd ask the child to move his head this way or that, or Vic would gently place his hand on the boy's head and place it in the correct position. At the end of the haircut, Vic would turn the chair so that the youngster would face the mirror and see that both ears were, indeed, still attached. The barber would splash a little cologne onto his hands and gently rub it onto the boy's neck, and he would even take out the hand vibrator to tickle the lad just a bit to get him to smile. Sometimes that worked. Frequently, though, when the boy's mother would walk into the shop to pick up her son and take him home, the child would run to the woman, throw his arms around her waist, and bury his face in her skirt. The mom, slightly perplexed, would smile faintly and then ask, "How was he?" To which Vic would simply reply, "He was an angel." Then the two would turn and walk slowly to the door saying nothing further. Richie felt sorry for the kid, figuring that the experience had probably shaved at least an inch or two of future growth off the young fellow's height.

Giving the barber a moment to remove the booster seat and put it aside, Richie stood up and went over to barber's chair, and bounding onto the foot rest said, "Hey, Vic!" The reply came, "Hey! Ah . . . ?" When the barber baked, Richie supplied his name. Recovering quickly, Vic said, "Richie. That's right." He then added, "Sorry, kid – faces I remember, names, not so well." With a wave of the hand Richie said, "Not a problem."

As Vic was setting everything up for the haircut, he began making small talk with Richie – tried to, at least.

"Where do you live, again?" Vic began.

"Just outside of town on Fair Oaks Drive," Richie told him.

"Oh," Vic said, "Over by the cemetery?"

"Actually, on the cemetery."

The barber paused in making his preparations and looked at Richie by way of the mirror. "You mean, next to the cemetery?" Vic asked to clarify.

"No. Our house is on cemetery property, just inside the gates."

Vic, securing the cloth around Richie's neck said, "Isn't that kind of spooky?"

"Quiet, maybe, but not spooky."

"But aren't you afraid at night? If I lived out there I'd shit my pants every time I heard a noise or thought I saw something moving in the dark."

"Really, it's peaceful all the time," Richie said. Then, deciding to play on the barber's fears just for fun he added, "Of course, we have a special patrol that goes around the perimeter at night looking for ghosts or the occasional undead. They're on foot and use infrared light so they don't disturb our live guests, but I could arrange for you to go out with them some night, if you'd like."

"Hell no!" Vic responded. "You're not going to get me to go on no spook hunt!"

"Okay," Richie said with a hint of a smirk, "I just thought I'd ask."

Vic went over to the counter and picked up his scissors and comb. As he did so, he muttered under his breath, "Spook hunt? Hell no! Those people must be nuts living on a cemetery!"

Walking behind Richie, Vic brought his arms up to start cutting when he suddenly realized that he didn't know what kind of haircut his client wanted. Still holding the scissors and comb, Vic placed his hands on Richie's shoulders and asked, "How do you want this cut?" Richie, feeling brave, said, "I just want a trim, Vic."

In the mirror the young man could see the barber's eyes narrow just a bit. "What are you," Vic finally asked, "one of those GD hippies?"

Richie replied, "No, my girlfriend said she'd like to see what I looked like if my hair was a little longer."

With that, Vic's attitude changed. With a smile he said, "A girlfriend, huh? Is she pretty?"

"Yes, very," Richie responded.

"Meet her in high school?"

"First day of class."

Vic was truly impressed and wanted to know what other possible conquests may have made themselves available to the young man. "So," he said, "at the end of the school day I'll bet there's lots of poontang cruising around out in the parking lot."

Familiar with the expression, having heard it flying around the locker room of the high school gym, Richie, nonetheless, detested the word – he thought it to be demeaning and crude, but considering the source of the question, he shouldn't have been surprised that it would be uttered. Still, Richie couldn't resist messing with the barber's mind one last time.

"Oh, I don't know, Vic," Richie said, "someone will have to point one out to me some day. All those Japanese cars look alike!"

Nine

The corporation that held the title to the building that Jon was interested in leasing had its headquarters on the east coast, hence, an absentee owner, which couldn't have been better suited for Jon's purpose. Because it was so far away, that type of owner was not interested in the day to day operation of whoever held the lease, as long as a check showed up at the beginning of each month in payment.

The absentee owner did not even bother to employ a local agent, but preferred, instead, to deal directly with the leaseholder. It thereby eliminated having to pay a monthly fee to what would only be, it was felt, a disinterested third party. Since the corporation would then rely on the leaseholder to adequately report on the condition of the building, and since the lease holder didn't feel it had to be too accurate with its assessment because the owner was on the other side of the country, the building was allowed to fall into a minor state of disrepair, appearing neglected and deserted – again, perfect for Jon's needs. Considering that the previous tenant had vacated the premises a couple of years before, with absolutely no work at all being performed on the building by the owner to correct deficiencies in its condition in the interim, only made things that much better as far as Jon was concerned.

It would seem that dealing with an absentee owner located three thousand miles away would pose a problem for Jon in gaining access to the building - but it didn't. Money, he knew, talked, and the more money available, the easier it was for mere dialogue to get whatever it was that you wanted. Being that Jon could tap the resources of one of the most powerful entities of the federal government, possessing a budget that was not only immense, but totally lacking in any requirement for accountability as well, also didn't hurt. Jon, in a phone call, did talk the talk, and offering an extremely enticing sum of money – cash always seemed to work better – was able to secure the lease without the necessity of an in-person meeting with a corporate official. The keys to the property were simply sent to him via parcel post.

"The setup couldn't be sweeter," Jon said over the speaker phone. Talking with his contact from The Agency (he preferred referring to it as "The Company", rather than, "The Agency"), Jon thought it wiser not to continue the conversation so openly. He picked up the phone's handset and turned off the speaker phone. "The place has looked deserted for years," Jon said, "even when it was in full operation. The windows are opaque, and from the outside, lighting appears to be very dim – no one can see what's going on inside, no matter how hard they try. We'll be in the rear portion of the building – we can set up a dark curtain to absorb any light and deaden any extraneous noise that might emanate from that section of the building – and it can be stretched across the entire area to cordon off the necessary workspace. That part of the structure was only used for storage, so there's no equipment that needs to be removed – and the floor is made out of concrete, so any material that might spill out during the transfer will be easy to clean up."

"How soon can you start receiving shipments?" The Company rep inquired.

"I don't see why we can't get things going by the end of next week," Jon replied. He then added, "I've already made some contingency plans for any delays we might encounter during the transfers, and as you know, we already have a cover story in the wings in case someone inadvertently discovers the operation."

"Then," The Company rep said, "you have a 'go' for the operation."

"We have a 'go'," Jon repeated.

Ten

Ellen June stood at the kitchen sink, arms in dishwater up to her elbows. The window set in the wall above the sink was open, and a fine, fresh breeze made its way indoors, much to Ellen's delight. She breathed deeply as the scent of newly mowed lawn came to her nose, and gazing at the lovely day that was unfolding outside, she thought that it would be just the perfect time to pickle watermelon rind or bury a loved one.

While Ellen was daydreaming with her hands still immersed in dishwater, Jon, and his dad, Samuel, walked into the kitchen.

"Oh! Good timing, guys," Ellen said as they entered. "The help has arrived!" She joyfully announced. "You can grab a towel, Jon, and start drying those dishes."

"Can't," Jon said. "I don't want to get dishpan hands, some of our customers might complain!"

"They're dead, Jon," Ellen said, stating the obvious. "And besides, you only get dishpan hands from washing dishes, not drying them."

"Oh well," Jon sighed, "it was worth a shot. Where's the dish towel?"

Ellen June, with hands still in water, merely gave a nod with her head to point Jon in the right direction, saying, "It's over in the pantry by the water heater, the same spot it's been in ever since we moved into this place!"

Jon's dad, Samuel, whispered in a voice loud enough for Ellen to hear from across the room, "Has Agent X 100 called yet?"

"Now Dad," Ellen said, "you have to knock off this business about working for the government." Shaking her head negatively, she looked at Sammy, a name she sometimes used in referring to her father-in-law, and was astonished by his steadfast persistence.

"Well, did he?" Jon's dad asked, whispering, ignoring the admonishment.

Ellen June looked over at Jon and mouthed the word "meds", inquiring of her husband if his father had remembered to take his pills. Jon simply shrugged his shoulders and raised his hands in a palm up gesture to indicate that he didn't know.

Finishing with the dishes, Ellen dried her hands and walked over to Sammy. She smiled at him sweetly and then gave him a hug. Looking at Jon she asked, "Any funerals this morning?" Jon answered, "No, but we do have one later at 5 o'clock. The family wanted a service around dusk."

Ellen June, ever buoyant said, "Well, that means I'm making pickled watermelon rind this morning!" She gently patted Jon's dad on the arm and then said, "First, though, since it's such a nice day outside, I think I'll go walk the graves. I haven't done that in a while."

Sammy suddenly asked, "Any cookies?"

Ellen June smiled and said, "They're in the cookie jar, Dad. I made a fresh batch this morning."

"Oh, boy!" Sammy responded. Going over to the counter, he took the lid off the cookie jar and gingerly pulled out a cookie, not wanting it to break apart before he was able to take his first bite.

"Well, you boys have fun," Ellen said, and with a wave of her hand she went out the door.

Now eating his cookie, Jon's dad moved over to the sink to watch through the open window as Ellen began her walk. When he was sure she was out of earshot, he turned to Jon and in a calm, coherent, mature voice of a completely capable senior citizen said, "Ellen June is such a lovely woman. I really hate deceiving her like this."

Eleven

"Walking the graves" was something that Ellen June had done from the time she was a little girl. She grew up in this business. Her family had a mortuary – a "funeral home" was what her parents preferred to call it – and from a very young age, Ellen was taught the importance of the service that they were providing to the community. She was told that what they did went beyond merely preparing the body for burial. Ellen June learned that what her family's business also was offering was an opportunity to assist the bereaved in the initial process of grieving. Frequently, there was a viewing of the body, but sometimes there was not. Always, however, the memorial service was held with dignity and respect for the deceased, and a genuine concern for the well-being of the grieving family.

Ellen would sometimes accompany her parents to the cemetery and explore the nearby graves while the service for the departed was in progress. Whenever she'd see the headstone of a person her family had interred, Ellen June felt a certain amount of pride for the comfort their funeral home had provided to the family of the deceased. Now, years later, she still felt the same self-satisfaction when thinking of how she and Jon were helping families during their time of need in almost exactly the same way.

Even though they'd only been operating this cemetery for a few years, Ellen still recognized some of the names scattered throughout the grave markers. Most she knew only as acquaintances in life, yet she felt a tinge of grief over their passing. The hardest area for her to walk through, however, was the section set aside for children. As a mother, she could only imagine the pain there was in losing a child – the agony of having an infant die a day or two after birth was one thing, but having what appeared to be a perfectly healthy toddler suddenly die for no apparent reason would surely be total devastation for any parent. She always shed a tear while walking the graves of these children and came away saying a silent prayer in the hopes that research would soon discover the cause of these terrible sudden deaths in children.

As Ellen June started walking back to the house to begin preparing the pickled watermelon rind, she suddenly thought of her sister, Shari. Ellen didn't believe in telepathy, but it certainly was strange the way she'd always receive a phone call from Shari within a day or two after her sister had unexpectedly cropped up in her mind. Ellen June wasn't entirely sure what caused these instantaneous thoughts to be triggered, either. Shari was childless, so Ellen didn't think her passing by the graves of the children was the reason why her sister had abruptly popped into her head. Perhaps, she supposed, it was because Ellen June had visited the grave of a frequently widowed woman who had finally succumbed years after burying the last of her seven husbands.

Shari, too, had had many husbands – five or six at last count as far as Ellen could remember – but Shari's long string of men had come about because of divorce, not from death. Shari's most recent husband (conquest, as Ellen June habitually put it to Jon) came into her life in a most unusual way.

One lovely Sunday morning, Shari was sitting in her breakfast nook, reading the newspaper while having tea and toast with marmalade. The day had started out peacefully and quiet, as her Sunday mornings usually were, when, all of a sudden, a 1958 Studebaker Hawk came crashing through the kitchen wall and miraculously stopped within an inch of the kitchen table. Thankfully, none of Shari's tea was spilt. Within a matter moments there was a polite knock on the back door, located down a short hallway from the kitchen. Shari went to the door and opened it. The mustached driver of the car was standing there, a straw dress hat in hand. Somehow he managed to look both pleasant and sleazy at the same time (it was probably because of all the grease that he had used to slick back his hair). Of course, Shari fell in love with him on the spot.

"Sorry about trying to give you a drive-thru kitchen," the man said with a smile that could have easily come from any used car salesman. "I was attempting to avoid running over a cat."

"Ooh!" Shari gushed. "An animal lover!"

Chuckling a bit, the driver said, "Hope I didn't spoil your morning."

"No," Shari said. "You didn't even make me spill my tea!" She furthered with a laugh.

"So, no harm done – that's good," the sleazebag responded, still sporting his obnoxious grin.

"You'll stay for breakfast, then?" She queried.

"Only if you can promise that I won't get a ticket for parking illegally!" He replied.

With that, they both laughed uproariously.

Strolling up to the house, Ellen was struggling to remember the date of her sister's wedding – it couldn't have been that long ago, she reasoned, maybe just a couple of months. Try as she might, though, Ellen June just couldn't remember when it took place.

"Must be having one of those senior moments," she mumbled under her breath. Thinking that her husband probably hadn't yet left the kitchen, Ellen shouted out to Jon as she opened the back door, "Honey, how long has Shari been married?"

Jon and his dad were still at the counter, Jon having a cup of coffee, Samuel eating a cookie and drinking milk. Jon had just taken a sip of coffee and swallowed hard when he heard Ellen June entering the kitchen, asking her question - as if her arrival had surprised him. Recovering a bit, and in an attempt to answer Ellen's question, Jon finally said, "Which time?"

"The last time, silly," she answered.

"Oh, you mean her marriage to the Studebaker Bomber - the guy that rammed into her kitchen wall?"

"That's the one."

"I think it's been about seven weeks," Jon said, "possibly a longevity record for your sister," he added.

"Be nice, Jon."

"I am being nice - it seems that Shari changes her marital status every time she has a mood swing."

"You know she's taking medication for that," Ellen said, defending her sister.

"Well, it's not strong enough, if you ask me."

"No one's asking you, Jon!"

"Any more cookies?" Sammy suddenly interjected, crumbs still sticking to the corners of his mouth.

Ellen June looked over at her father-in-law, and giggling, asked, "Dad, did you eat all of those cookies?"

"He ate more!" Sammy said with a deadpan expression, pointing to his son.

Ellen glanced at her husband. Without saying a word, Jon held up one finger. When Ellen June narrowed her eyes and gave Jon a severe look, he reluctantly held up a second finger.

"You two have probably spoiled your appetite for dinner," she said.

"What's for dinner?" Sammy quickly asked.

Ellen June rolled her eyes towards the ceiling and shook her head in disbelief, but still let out with a chuckle.

"Getting back to your sister," Jon said, "why did you want to know how long she's been married to the sleazebag?"

"I know you don't like the guy, Jon, but do you have to refer to him with that term?" Ellen replied.

"Pot roast?" The elder Jung abruptly threw into the mix.

"What?" Ellen June asked, fully not expecting that question.

"Maybe pot roast tonight?" Jon's father asked.

"Honestly, Dad," Ellen said, again with a giggle, "You're a bottomless pit!"

"And your sister?" Jon inquired.

"No, I think her appetite is . . . . " Ellen June said, then paused and corrected herself. "You mean, why did I want to know how long she's been married?"

"This time?" Jon asked to be clear.

"Yes, this time," Ellen said. "Well, she continued, "I was walking by the grave of that woman that had been widowed so many times . . . "

"The one with the grave marker that reads 'Dean Witter Merrill Lynch Morgan Stanley Rockefeller?'" Jon quickly asked.

"Come on," Ellen said, "you know the marker only has one last name."

"Yeah, but that was one rich widow!"

"Anyway," Ellen forcefully said, trying to put the conversation back on track, "seeing the grave of that woman who had so many husbands naturally made me think of my sister – and how strange it is that she always calls within a day or two after I think of her – and how I honestly couldn't remember how long she's been married, and that's why I asked you when I came into the house – and, wait . . . isn't that the phone ringing? It is! I'll bet it's Shari!" With that, Ellen June dashed out of the room.

"Sometimes that woman is like a fart in the wind," Jon commented to the empty space where his wife had been standing, "she's all over the place."

"Did I mention that Ellen really does make a good cookie?" Jon's father asked while wiping the crumbs away from his mouth.

"Yes, I think you did."

"You know, Son, we almost got caught with our hand in the cookie jar, so to speak. With this new program about to start, we'll have to have safeguards in place so that Ellen June doesn't accidentally stumble across anything that even hints at the true nature of this operation simply because we've been lax and overlooked something – there could be some serious repercussions if she does."

"As long as she still thinks you're living out your second childhood, I don't think we'll have any problems."

"I'm not so sure," Samuel said, "I think she's more astute than she lets on."

"After seeing her last act, I have my doubts about that. Besides, I think she's starting to have problems with her short term memory."

"Still, we need to take precautions."

"I agree," Jon said. He then added, "You know, Dad, my sweet tooth is kicking in again – any more cookies in the jar?"

"I believe there is one left," Samuel said.

"Could you pass it to me, please?"

"Get your own damn cookie!" Jon's dad shot back with a smile.

Suddenly, a scream from Ellen June came from down the hall. Jon and his dad looked at each other with some concern, but the scream, they decided, wasn't one of alarm, but rather was issued in response to something that portend excitement and expectation.

"I told you so!" Ellen yelled out to Jon and Sammy as she came running back towards the kitchen. "And you didn't believe me!"

"Didn't believe what?" Jon bluntly asked when his wife rushed into the room.

"The Queen! The Queen!" Ellen June gushed with unbridled enthusiasm. "Shari called to tell me that The Queen's Royal Flight will be passing through this area within a matter of days!"

"Why would The Queen of England be visiting this part of the United States?" Jon wondered out loud.

"She's here to see Indians," Ellen replied.

"Doesn't she have plenty of folks from the Punjab back in her own country?"

"Not India Indians, Jon - Native Americans – it seems The Queen is fascinated by their culture."

"Somehow, I can't picture that woman wearing a headdress and moccasins," Jon remarked.

"She likes the Native American earthenware, with their colorful, unique designs," Ellen redirected.

"I can't imagine any of that ever being used at Buckingham Palace, either," Jon replied.

"Maybe she needs plates to serve cookies!" Sammy quickly added.

Ellen June gave Jon's father a bemused look. "Anyway," she finally said to her husband, "the Royal Flight will be coming through this area as it heads back to Black Rock air base after The Queen visits the Indian reservation."

"Thunderbirds?" Jon wanted to know.

"What?" Ellen said in a puzzled response.

"Will this be a flight of Thunderbirds?" Jon asked. "You know, those big mythological Indian birds," he added for clarification.

"No – helicopters, I believe," Ellen June said.

"God save The Queen!" Samuel suddenly uttered with genuine concern.

"Yeah, I don't like helicopters either," Jon quickly chimed in, matter-of-factly.

Ellen gave both men a disgruntled look. "Honestly, you two!" She said. Then, with mounting excitement Ellen June continued by saying, "I just know that The Queen is going to stop by any day now – it's destiny! So, please, keep the bathroom tidy! Staring at Jon and pointing at him at the same time she added, "And you - get those girlie magazines out of there!"

Jon decided, perhaps unwisely, to ignore Ellen June's command, choosing, instead, to answer with, "I know those helicopters are large enough to have toilets that will accommodate any Royal arse, so I doubt that they'll need to stop here."

"Jon!" Ellen fired back, her patience running thin.

"Okay," he said, succinctly, recognizing when it was time for him to shut up.

Twelve

Jon pulled the black sedan into the driveway of the house after he had supervised the funeral of a local dignitary. Ordinarily, his number two man would oversee most of the services, but with the importance of this type of funeral, Jon felt he should take the duty. He really didn't mind officiating since it kept his hand in the game and allowed him to track what was going on in the community.

Sometimes, however, the professional requirements of the job were irksome to Jon. He fully understood the need to drive away from the grave site in the sedan after the service (Jon didn't think it would look dignified if he walked to the house while wearing a suit). Still, the drive always seemed awkward to him, because he only had a short distance to go. Jon could also see the professional necessity of performing his duties in business attire. Just the same, he could hardly wait to get out of his suit when he got home and put on some casual clothes.

While getting out of the car, Jon saw Richie walking towards the house from the front gate. In a moment of parental pride, he acknowledged to himself that his son was turning into a fine young man, and that put a smile onto Jon's face. He waved to Richie and decided to wait for him before going into the house. As the youth drew nearer, Jon called out, "Where have you been, Son?"

"I went to the Scottish Games," Richie replied.

When his son reached the car, Jon put his arm around the boy's shoulder. Together, they walked up onto the porch.

"Did you see them throw those big poles?" Jon inquired.

"Yep, I sure did," Richie said, "but darn if they don't look more like shrunken telephone poles to me."

"I agree," Jon responded as they stopped at the front door. "But the way they can pick them up, cradle the end in their hands, and then toss them as if they were small 2 by 4s – it's amazing!"

Richie excitedly grabbed his dad by the arm and said, "Someone got brained today!"

"Oh, no!" Jon replied with a nervous laugh.

"The guy wasn't' hurt that bad – when the end of the pole landed on the ground and it started to fall, he got his arms up into the air and they took most of the blow," Richie told his father. "But I still think he's going to have a bump on his head," he added.

"It sounds as though we could have had another customer," Jon said with a smile as he opened the front door and they went inside.

"I'm back!" Richie announced to the empty room.

"Me too!" Jon added while he closed the door.

Ellen walked into the living room from the kitchen, followed by Jon's dad. She went over to Jon, greeted him, and then kissed him on the cheek. Turning to her son, she hugged him as she said hello. She then asked, "Did you have fun at the Scottish Games?"

"He saw some guy get bashed in the head with a telephone pole!" Jon replied before his son could answer.

"Actually," Richie quickly added before his dad could say more, "it was a little smaller than that, but not by much."

"Oh, the poor fellow," Ellen June said, sympathetically.

"He's all right, though" Richie replied. "The guy's as big as an ox. I think all those Scots are born with extra thick skulls!"

"It must be from all of that haggis that they eat," Jon offered.

"Or maybe it's from eating cookies!" Sammy exclaimed.

"That has to be better than haggis!" Richie acknowledged.

"What isn't?" Jon added.

Ellen, however, had a different opinion. "I've heard that haggis is an interesting dish," she said in all honesty. "I think I'd like to try it someday."

Richie looked at his mother in disbelief and said, "Are you kidding? It sounds disgusting! Liver, heart, and oatmeal boiled in the stomach of a sheep, I wonder what spices have to been added to keep down the gag reflex while you're trying to eat that thing?"

"Still, it might be interesting to try," Ellen again suggested.

"I thought we were having pot roast tonight," Sammy quickly offered.

Ellen smiled at her father-in-law and patted him on the forearm. "Even so, Dad, I'd like to make haggis for dinner sometime," she calmly admitted.

Without skipping a beat, Samuel said, "Count me out!"

"I think I smelled it once out at the Games," Jon said. "The aroma was kind of a cross between a butcher's shop, candy store, and an open sewer. Appetizing would not be how I would describe it!"

Hearing this, Ellen June frowned a bit as she looked at her son and said, "I guess you're not game, either?"

"Sorry, but no," Richie replied. "I do like the word though, Mom."

"What? Ellen June responded.

"The sound of the word."

"What word?" She repeated, a little confused.

"Haggis!" Richie said with a little laugh. "Isn't that a great name for a dog?"

"Well . . . ?" Ellen replied without committing herself further.

Richie merely smiled at his mom and said, "Maybe in a few years I'll have two sheep herding dogs. One I'll call Robby. The other will be called Haggis! We'd never herd any sheep, but we'd do everything else together. Don't you think those would be great names for my dogs?" Richie eagerly asked.

Hoping not to hurt her son's feelings, Ellen demurely replied, "Actually, to me they sound more like names for a couple of auto mechanics."

Jon walked over to Ellen June. Taking pity on her because no one was willing to support her to at least try this foul sounding dish, he said, "OK, let's suppose that you actually went ahead and made this mess one day. What would you do with it if none of us ate it?"

"Give it to a sheep herding dog?" Richie offered as a suggestion.

"I doubt if they'd even eat it," Jon quickly said, "they'd think they were being punished!"

Ellen June, having no suitable answer, at first feebly said, "Bury it?" But then, upon reflection, she couldn't actually come up with a better answer, so Ellen grimaced a bit and finally said, "Well, Dad, it looks like we'll be having pot roast from here on out!"

"Yippee!" Sammy gleefully responded, then added, "and meat load, too?"

"I guess," Ellen glumly said.

Jon patted her shoulder in support, "Maybe someday it will happen," he said.

"Yeah, the same day my prince shows up!" Ellen June replied.

Just to change the subject Jon turned to his son and said, "Say! Didn't you go out to the Games with that pretty little filly?"

Suddenly, Ellen, a tad bit irritable after her lost battle over the haggis, chimed in, "Susan! That's her name! Call her Susan!"

"Okay," Jon hesitantly replied, "Didn't you go with that pretty little filly named *Susan*?"

Ellen June gave her husband the dirtiest look.

Disregarding the minor tension going on between his parents, Richie said, "Yep, she's the one I took."

"How did she like it?" Jon asked.

"Well, she's seen the Games before – so she was happy just to show me around."

Jon knew that with so much to see at the Scottish Games, Richie had to have a favorite. "Out of everything going on at the Games, what did you like the best," he asked his son.

Without hesitating, Richie, with complete certainty, quickly exclaimed, "The bagpipes!"

"Once again, we have an encounter with a sheep's stomach!" Jon responded.

"Actually not, Dad. Animal hides were originally used, but the bag of the modern day bagpipe is now usually made out of a synthetic material."

"Oh, good," Jon said, "that way they can save the stomach for haggis!"

Richie chuckled at his dad. "You know, the pipes are really an interesting instrument to play."

"Is that a fact?" Jon said with an inquisitive smile. "Then please, oh wondrous one, enlighten us!"

"Well, many people think that the piper actually plays the notes from air being blown into the mouthpiece."

"And that's not the case?" Jon inquired.

"No. The piper uses the mouthpiece to blow air into the bag. Then, squeezing the bag, he creates the notes by placing his fingers on the different holes of the chanter when the air pushes past a reed."

"Wouldn't that make you lightheaded, blowing into the mouthpiece all the time?"

"I'm sure there must be a technique to keep that from happening. That's what I need to find out."

"So," Jon said, " you really want to play this thing?"

"Yes, if I can build up my lung capacity," Richie replied.

Jon, fishing around for what sounded to him like Zen philosophy said, "Be the windbag!"

"Wait!" Richie replied, "You studied Eastern religion. Who was your master?"

"It was either Arthur Treacher or Arthur Murray," Jon said, I can't remember which."

Realizing it was neither, but appreciating his father's humor, Richie smiled and said, "Can we return to the topic of discussion?"

"Being?'

"Bagpipes!"

"Oh, yes. Please do," Jon replied.

Richie looked over to his mom and grandfather, hoping they wouldn't mind if he dominated a little more of the conversation. They both nodded their heads, encouraging the young man to continue.

Being so enthusiastic about the subject, Richie eagerly resumed his narrative. "Well," he said, "besides having an interesting sound, I like the pipes because they have a fascinating history. They're so loud, they can be heard more than a mile away. Armies have used pipes for centuries to march troops into battle. They were even utilized during World War Two!"

"I wonder how well bagpipes stood up to a German rifle bullet or machine gun fire." Jon queried.

"Probably about as well as human flesh," Richie somberly replied.

After a moment's reflection Jon said, "You do realize, Son, that you'll have to wear a kilt when you play the pipes – it's tradition."

"I wouldn't mind," Richie offered.

"You gonna wear anything under the kilt?"

"I don't know, yet."

"That's the age ole question, isn't it?" Jon posed. "What does a Scot wear beneath his kilt?"

"Unless the wind rustles his kilt, one will never know, will they?" Richie responded.

"Still," Jon replied, "when that cold wind whistles up the old kilt, it can get pretty nippy down there! Why do you think you hear the term "hoot man!" so often when a blast of freezing air breaches the underside of a kilt?"

"OK – you've convinced me. I'll wear a pair of plaid boxer shorts underneath – nice and conservative!"

"Good choice!" Jon offered.

"Besides, Susan says I have the legs for it."

Ellen quickly entered the conversation and suddenly interjected, "How would she know?"

"Swimming suits! Remember?" Richie said in his defense. He then added, "We have gone to the pool together."

"That's right," Ellen June said somewhat satisfied with the answer, but meddling further she also added, "but, is that the only time?"

"Yes, Mother, that's the only time."

"Good," Ellen said in relief. She continued with, "Oh, Richie, when you wore shorts as a boy, you had the cutest little legs!"

"They're hairy, now!" Sammy said in an unsolicited comment, briefly rejoining the discussion.

Ellen looked at her father-in-law and merely sighed. "Come on, Dad," she finally said, "let's get started on the pot roast. You can cut the carrots."

"Oh boy!" Sammy excitedly responded.

Thirteen

It was black deception, as simple as that. A ruse planted in plain sight, having utilitarian function not quite defined which masked the true sinister intent built into its disguise. Jon had arranged to have the long, narrow trailer quietly parked at the edge of the road near the abandoned nondescript building in the middle of the night. One day, the spot was empty. The next, the trailer had simply appeared.

Since the portion of the road on which the trailer was parked terminated with a dead end, there wasn't any passing traffic to speak of - either vehicular or pedestrian. But for the curious that traversed the twenty or thirty yards beyond the curve of the adjoining active roadway for a glance, the cloaking efforts successfully served to confuse.

Approaching the trailer end which coupled to a truck, a flexible hose with a six inch diameter could be observed attached near the bottom, joining with a smooth hose of a slightly smaller diameter that had been placed along the gutter. On the left side of that front end, a small set of stairs led up to a walkway that went to the back of the trailer. A metal wall bordered the right side of the narrow non-slip path, a short handrail ran along its course on the left. At the end of the walkway was another set of taller steps that led up to a platform, also enclosed by a guardrail that lined its perimeter. The platform, no doubt, was to allow for observation – but the observation of what? From there an eyewitness would be overlooking a roof. Was purposeful deceit set in place?

At the back end of the trailer, another flexible hose of six inch diameter was connected to a fixture just below the roof line. The hose was coiled and fastened to the end wall, clearly not long enough to reach the ground, with the detached terminus blatantly exposed to the open air. Was this camouflage meant to amuse? Gotcha!

The coup de grace of this fraudulent staging appeared on the bottom of the trailer running just below the walkway. Three evenly spaced portals, looking very much like the hatches on the torpedo tubes of a WW II submarine, were secured in the closed position by a series of formidable looking latches. Each door had a placard that warned about the danger of high pressure containment. An additional cautionary placard also prohibited their opening by unauthorized personnel. A similar door, which sealed the tube, could be opened on the opposite side – was this a perfect way to transport bodies, perhaps? Now poised, with a plan of deception, the operation could confidently begin.

Fourteen

On a fine spring morning a single engine airplane, about ten miles southeast of the local airport, made a radio call to the tower for landing instructions. The air traffic was light, so the pilot was issued a brief clearance for the main runway.

"Bonanza One Tango Victor, Black Rock tower, straight-in runway 32. Wind, three one zero degrees at 7. Altimeter, 29 point 97. Report 3 mile final. Over."

The pilot acknowledged by repeating, "Straight-in runway 32. Report three mile final. One Tango Victor. Over."

"And One Tango Victor – traffic, 9 o'clock at 3000 feet, also northwest bound - a flight of four Royal Air Force helicopters. You won't be able to monitor their radio calls unless you're UHF capable. I'll keep you advised of any change in their altitude or heading. Over."

The Bonanza pilot was curious and inquired, "What's the RAF doing in this part of the U.S. – joint maneuvers?"

"No, believe it or not, sightseeing!" Black Rock replied.

"Ok – One Tango Victor is looking. Correction, One Tango Victor has the traffic in sight. Over."

On board The Queen's Flight – a large Sea King helicopter – an enlisted man, serving as The Queen's military adjutant – came forward to the cockpit to speak to the pilot. Leaning in close so that he could be heard above the noise of the engines he said, "Major, Her Majesty is in need of the rotorcraft's commode."

"Well, Corporal," the pilot said, "point out the facility and lead Her Grace to it."

"Sir, I was going to do just that, but as you'll remember, the toilet is inoperative and has been placed off limits with that yellow crime scene tape."

"Oh, yes – inoperative," the Major said. Slightly embarrassed he added, "I'm afraid that tape is a bit tacky, is that – however, it was the best we could do under the circumstances. The Americans didn't have anything else that seemed regal or elegant enough for the task!"

"Quite!"

"Hawkins," the pilot continued, "go back and inform Her Majesty that we'll be landing soon."

"I've mentioned that, Sir, but The Queen says that she *really* has to go. She's already started doing a potty dance in front of the commode door!"

"We're in a real pickle here, Corporal. The Royal Flush is broken on the command ship and none of the other rotorcrafts have a toilet on board."

"Can't we just land and find a place that has a facility that The Queen can use?"

"That might pose a security problem, unless . . . ," the major said, pausing to think for a moment, then picking up with, "unless we can find an area that's somewhat isolated."

Looking through the cockpit window for a suitable site, the corporal quickly discovered a promising landing zone for the helicopters.

Pointing out the spot to the major, Hawkins said, "What about down there, Sir – off to the left – about a mile ahead? There's a large area of green with a few solitary buildings."

"I think that's just the ticket, Corporal! Spot on! I'll contact ATC and tell them that we're going to divert."

Moments later, the airport's tower made a transmission to advise the single engine pilot of the change of plans for the Royal Flight.

"Bonanza One Tango Victor, Black Rock tower. Those RAF helicopters are no longer a factor – seems there was an urgent need for an unscheduled landing a few miles from the airport. Over."

The pilot and the tower then informally exchanged a possible reason for the Royal Flight's diversion.

"Late for tea?"

"Or something like that!"

Fifteen

Not too far from the caretaker's house, a crew was digging a grave in a section near the cemetery's property line. An outcropping of small buildings was nearby, containing a small temporary morgue, a tool shed, and a garage for the hearse. Adjacent to the buildings was a parcel of unimproved land that was being held in reserve for future expansion. About the size of a football field, that portion of land was perfectly flat, had sparse vegetation, no trees, no overhanging power lines or other obstructions – in short, it was an ideal spot to set down a flight of helicopters. There was very little wind that morning so the pilot of the lead rotorcraft decided to make his landing approach to the field heading towards the isolated buildings.

Billy Joe Bob was on the backhoe, just beginning his work. While using the coordinated application of two levers as he started to dig the grave, he looked up and saw the RAF helicopters descending. "What the heck?" Billy Joe Bob said out loud. From his position, he noticed that the pilot of one of the smaller rotorcrafts about to touch down could easily be observed making hand movements on levers in the cockpit of the helicopter that were very similar, at least in Billy Joe Bob's mind, to those he was using while operating the backhoe.

He let out with a laugh and then started giving the pilot instructions on his landing technique. "That a boy," he said, "a little more to the right – lower, lower, you're almost down." Billy Joe Bob laughed again. Moving the levers of his backhoe he called out to one of his co-workers, "Hey Lenny, Look! I could land a helicopter!"

"Yeah," Lenny responded, "if you tried to land a helicopter the same way you operate a backhoe, you'd still end up digging a hole in the ground big enough for a grave!"

With all four rotorcraft on the ground, engines shutdown and rotors slowly rotating to a stop, a detachment of six Royal Marines casually clambered down the airstair door of The Queen's aircraft. They smartly marched to positions interspersed around the helicopter, turned outward from the craft and then snapped to attention.

With The Queen pausing at the door of the helicopter, ready to depart the craft, she shouted to the pilot, "That's all right, Major. I don't need all of these marines – we don't want to alarm the Colonist and make them think this is an invasion! No – Hawkins here and I will be just fine on our own." The Queen looked at the young man and with a motherly smile said, "Won't we, Son?"

"Yes, Ma'am!" The Corporal replied in a military cadence.

Her Royal Highness held out her hand so that the marine could guide her down the steps and out of the helicopter. "Come on, Corporal," she said, "let's have an adventure, shan't we? Lead me to the door of the domicile."

"Certainly, Your Grace!"

After dismounting the stairs, the corporal turned and helped The Queen as she took her last step to the ground. Moving to the side of the monarch and slightly to the front, he extended his left arm forward, and pointing in the general direction they would be moving said, "Shall we proceed?"

The Queen simply responded with, "Let's!"

The Royal and the adjutant took a step or two towards the service buildings, and then turned to walk behind the structures to arrive at an open area off to the left, just past the last building.

"From the air, just before we touched down, I believe I saw a small garden and a pathway leading to a door of a house," the corporal said.

"Oh, I do love gardens!" The Queen announced.

"I think it's probably a tiny patch of vegetables, Your Grace."

"Still, it *is* a garden!"

Knowing not to question the monarch, the adjutant replied with, "Yes, Ma'am."

Turning right at the end of the buildings, the pair came to a driveway that led up to the service buildings. Crossing the driveway, they arrived at the edge of a lawn with stepping stones leading diagonally to a house, off to the left. After traversing the stepping stones, they came to a gravel walkway that ran parallel to the house. Visible a little further along, near the front of the house, there was a large shade tree with leaves that simmered in the light breeze. Across from the house, to their right, was a well-tended vegetable garden. An adjacent hedge, located straight ahead of them, ran along the garden's furthest edge, providing some welcomed privacy.

"Well," The Queen said, "isn't this nice?"

"Very nice, Your Grace."

"I wonder if they're English," The Queen pondered with a perfectly natural assumption.

"Perhaps, Ma'am," Hawkins responded.

Walking towards the door the corporal announced, "This appears not to be the main entrance, Your Majesty."

"Well," The Queen observed, "there's another pathway up ahead that leads beyond the garden. Shall we venture forth?"

"Yes," the corporal said, "I believe that will take us closer to the main entrance." He hesitated for a moment and then added, "With you permission, Your Grace, I need to be directly in front of you for your protection."

"Oh, bosh!" The Queen uttered. "There's not a soul around!"

"Still, our view to the front is obstructed by that hedge and I am sworn to protect you – so, Your Grace, if I have your permission, I will move to the front of you."

"Oh, very well Corporal, if you must. Carry on!"

With The Queen now in tow, the young marine moved gingerly along the path as it curved its way gently to the front of the house. An expanse of lawn covered the rest of the property which bordered a nearby auxiliary road. Across the road there was another section of lawn with a few scattered shade trees planted randomly to keep the routinely flat ground from looking so lonely and stark.

"See," The Queen said, "not a soul to be found - and it's so quiet."

"Actually, Your Grace, there might be a soul or two about," the corporal commented.

"How can that be?" The Queen asked. "I don't see a solitary person."

"Perhaps you've noticed those indentations in the grass over there? Those are grave markers."

Her Royal Highness was quiet for a moment, as if stunned by what she had just heard. She finally asked, "We're on a cemetery?"

"Yes, that's right, Your Grace."

"Fancy that! No wonder it's so quiet!"

"That it is, Ma'am."

The Queen turned to look at the house and said, "What a queer place for a home."

"There should be no problem with noisy neighbors," the corporal responded.

"I should hope not!"

Continuing on the pathway, the marine conjectured, "We should be very near the front door."

"Excellent," The Queen gushed, "'cause I've really got to go!"

Finally, coming to the short set of stairs that led to the porch, the corporal bounded up the steps, turned slightly and offered his hand to The Queen. Extending her right hand to the marine, The Queen took her left hand and hiked up her dress a little to help her to more easily negotiate the steps.

Walking to the door The Queen excitedly asked, "Oh, can I ring the doorbell?"

The marine wisely replied, "Certainly, Your Grace."

When the doorbell rang, Jon's dad was in the living room reading a news magazine. Ellen June was in the kitchen baking, well, what else?

"Dad," Ellen said, "would you mind getting the door?"

"Sure!" He then added, "Oh, are the cookies done yet?"

"Dad! Just get the door!"

Walking from the couch, Jon's dad crossed the room, grabbed the doorknob, and quickly opened the door. Seeing the woman standing at the doorway with the marine, he broke into a large grin.

"Hi, Queenie!" Jon's father said in a casual and overly friendly fashion.

"Sammy!" The Queen returned, surprised.

Jon's dad brought his right hand up to his mouth and put his index finger vertically to his lips. He then winked.

"Who is it, Dad?" Ellen June called out from the kitchen.

"I think it's The Queen," Sammy said, smiling at the monarch.

As she walked into the room, drying her hands on her apron, Ellen June instantly recognized Her Royal Highness and stopped dead in her tracks, overwhelmed. "Oh my juniper berries!" Ellen uttered. Stammering a little, embarrassed from this awkward initial reaction, she then tried to curtsey, and immediately fainted.

"Oh, the poor woman," The Queen said as gravity drew Ellen June to the floor.

Everyone momentarily stood in bemused silence, and then Her Majesty took charge. "Hawkins, quick – get some water!" The Queen ordered.

"Yes, Your Grace," the corporal said. Hesitating, he then asked, "Where?"

The Queen looked at Jon's father.

"Down the hall, Son, last door on the left hand side," Samuel Jung directed.

When the young marine disappeared down the hall, Jon's dad bowed his head reverently and said, "Your Majesty."

The Queen extended her hand, smiled and said, "Samuel."

"The last time I saw you, Your Grace, you were still a princess."

"Sometimes I wish I had never become queen," Her Royal Highness offered in all honesty. "And you," she continued, "were with the OSS the last time we met."

Nodding his head, Samuel said with a smile, "We won the war, didn't we?"

The Queen likewise nodded her head affirmatively and then asked, "Retired?"

"Nearly," Jon's dad said.

"And your son still works with you?"

"Ever since the latter part of the war."

"The cemetery – a nice cover!" The Queen commented.

"Yes, it's functional – profitable, too," Samuel admitted.

"How lovely!" The Queen acknowledged.

Just then, the corporal came walking back into the room.

"The water, Your Grace," the Royal Marine said, holding out a small plastic cup.

Putting her hand up, indicating that she wanted the corporal to wait for her instructions, The Queen then addressed Jon's dad.

"What's your daughter's name?"

"Daughter-in-law," Samuel gently corrected.

"Oh! But I bet she's like a daughter to you?"

"Very much so, Your Grace. She answers to Ellen or Ellen June – either one."

"Lovely names, Samuel," The Queen said with a smile. Turning to the corporal she then instructed, "Sprinkle some water on her face, Hawkins. But please, gently."

As the marine used his fingers to drop a small amount of water onto Ellen's face, Her Majesty began calling her name.

"Ellen. Ellen June. Come on, Dear. Wake up."

Ellen remained reclining on the floor, exhibiting no hint of a response.

"Had I been born a prince, perhaps I could wake her with a kiss?" The Queen offered with a smile.

Turning toward the marine she said, "Once again, Corporal. And remember, Son, be gentle."

"Yes, Ma'am."

Her Majesty held up her hand once again, indicating to the young man that she wanted him to wait. "On my command," she said as she, not too gingerly, sat down on the floor next to Ellen June, her Royal Legs bent and tucked up against her Royal Buttocks. Taking hold of the supine woman's hand, The Queen looked over at the Royal Marine, and with a simple nod of her head, instructed him to begin applying more water. Delicately stroking the hand of Samuel's daughter-in-law, the monarch implored the woman to arise as water droplets were placed upon her face.

"Ellen," The Queen quietly said as she continued to lightly stoke the woman's hand. "Wake up, Ellen June," she coaxed. "Come on, Dear. Wake up."

Ellen began to stir. With her cognitive abilities being restored, slowly at first and then with accelerating rapidity, Ellen June abruptly remembered whom she happened to be in the room with, and suddenly bolted upright.

"Holy hollyhocks!" Ellen said, now sitting on the floor next to The Queen. "Your Grace! You came! The loo!"

"Oh my word! I almost forgot!" The Queen said, now appearing extremely uncomfortable. Yet, the monarch still inquired, "What led you to believe that I would ever come here?"

"I simply knew it would happen one day!"

"Clairvoyance, that's wonderful, Dear — but I really have a pressing need right now!"

"Oh, I'm so glad we've been keeping it tidy for you!"

"Ellen June!" The Queen said. With clinched teeth she added, "Don't make me do a potty dance!"

"Your Grace! Please forgive my manners!" Ellen said to The Royal. Then, looking over to her father-in-law said, "Dad! Help Her Majesty to her feet!"

Offering The Queen his hand, Sammy assisted the monarch in getting up from her sitting position on the floor.

"This way, Queenie," Sammy said, leading Her Royal Highness away. "Oh," he added, "when you're through, maybe Ellen will give us a cookie!"

"Dad!" Ellen exclaimed to her father-in-law in disbelief. Still on the floor, Ellen June buried her face in the crook of her arm, trying to hide her embarrassment. "Cookies! Cookies! Cookies!" She moaned, "Why must it always be cookies!"

"Actually, Ma'am, The Queen loves cookies," the Royal Marine offered. "In fact, she just bought an earthenware plate at an Indian reservation to serve them at Buckingham Palace."

"Oh, no," Ellen June dejectedly said. With her face still buried in the crook of her arm she added, "I give up!" Raising her right arm so that it rested on its elbow, and moving her hand slowly back and forth, she said, "Where's the white flag so that I can wave it in capitulation?"

Sixteen

Standing in front of a full length mirror in a clothing store that sold Scottish apparel, Richie, peering at his image appearing in the mirror, was trying to make an honest assessment about what he saw.

"Before, I thought I'd be alright wearing this thing, but now, I'm not so sure," he said to his girlfriend, Susan, who was standing next to the mirror. Wanting her honest opinion, Richie asked, "Does this kilt make me look like a girl?"

Susan, with a slight smirk on her face, stepped over to her boyfriend, placed her right hand on his upper left arm, and gently pushed him out of the way. Moving in front of the mirror, she looked at Richie while pointing to her image. "*That's* what a girl looks like!" She proudly proclaimed. Turning to reveal her profile she added, "See, bumps in the sweater. You don't have those."

Moving closer to her, Richie lightly put his hands on his girlfriend's shoulders and directed her out of the way. Once again, standing before the mirror he said, "Thanks for the anatomy lesson, which I don't need, by the way." Susan smiled, coyly. Richie, continuing, said, "What I meant was, is the kilt at all girlish?" Striking a beauty contestant pose, Susan cleared her throat to get Richie's full attention, and then ran her hands down the side of her body to accentuate the curves that he didn't have. Raising her hands above her head, Susan simply exclaimed, "TA DA!"

Richie lowered his head, closed his eyes, and slowly shook his head negatively over his inability to adequately express his concerns.

The girl smiled sweetly. "Oh, Richie," Susan said with a little giggle, "are you asking if the kilt will make you look effeminate?"

Saying nothing, Richie merely nodded his head in the affirmative.

"Heck no!" Susan forcefully said. "Haven't I always told you that you have strong, muscular legs?"

"I suppose," Richie offered, now looking over at his girlfriend.

"Sure I have!" Susan said, reassuringly. In jest she added, "Of course, your kilt better have some pretty manly colors, otherwise people are going to think you're a girl!"

Richie hung his head again, shaking it negatively. This time, however, he had a gentle smile on his face.

"I don't know about the black and brown being together, though, they're kind of bland," she told him. "Are those the colors that you picked?"

"No," Richie replied. "I just took this kilt off the rack to see if this size would fit. We're mostly of German heritage, so I guess I can choose from the tartans of any clan. I was thinking of either black and red or black and green."

"Those are pretty bold colors," Susan said. "Bold enough, I mean."

"I could go with lavender and pink," Richie said with a wink," but those colors belong to the McLiberace's!"

His girlfriend giggled.

"My old man was right, though."

"How so?"

"These things are drafty! I noticed that from just walking around the store. We're barely into spring and it's still a little cool, but I can imagine what it's going to be like wearing this thing with a cold wind blowing between my legs. Just think what it's going to be like with a hefty wind-chill factor during the winter!"

"Hoot, man!" Susan exclaimed.

Richie let out with a laugh. "Good one," he said.

"Now you know what it's like to wear a 'mini'" Susan said. She then added, "At least on cold days I can put on tights!"

"Chicken!" Richie directed towards his girlfriend with a smile. "I thought plaid boxer shorts would be good enough to wear," he said, "but when it gets cold I guess I'll have to go shopping for some fur lined underwear!"

Seventeen

Thumbing through the day's mail, Ellen June came across a picture postcard of Buckingham Palace. Wondering who might have sent the card, Ellen turned it over to read:

Hello Dear,

Thank you so much for the use of the loo – it was nice and tidy! You can't have imagined how relieved I was to have found one! The earthenware plate I bought at the Indian reservation is a big hit at Buckingham Palace! Thanks also for the delicious cookies! If you are ever in London, please do drop by for a visit – I'd love to see you again.

Your,

Elizabeth II

P.S.
My very best to Sammy!

Well, Ellen June was so proud about the card that her seams were about to burst! *Imagine! The Queen of England writing to me!* Ellen thought. She could hardly wait to tell Jon, but he was out supervising a funeral and wasn't likely to return home any time soon. So, for now, she had to be content with the mere knowledge that she had been the recipient of a postcard written by the hand of the English monarch herself! Ellen picked up the card and read it once again. She smiled smugly, since she was a stickler for etiquette, and was satisfied that The Queen truly did have good manners because she had remembered to send a note of thanks. Still, however, Ellen June had to pinch herself to be sure that the postcard was real.

The funeral that Jon was overseeing was running smoothly. The service was for a Mason of the Scottish Rite – a ceremony with some pomp, but quietly dignified. Jon had worked hard in overcoming a potential problem that might have sent the Masons to another cemetery for their final interment: there were no granite headstones.

From the onset, the memorial park had decided to have flat bronze grave markers because they would allow for easier maintenance of the lawn - a lawnmower could cut the grass that bordered a flat marker without any additional maneuvering. The traditional headstone that jutted out of the ground, on the other hand, required extra labor for removing the grass that surrounded the markers.

For Masons, however, their Order's early foundation was based upon the skills they displayed in the carving of stone and the construction of buildings in brick or stone. These in-ground markers left no room for the talent of modern masonry to create the finely crafted headstones to proudly mark their graves. Jon's solution to the dilemma was simple: set aside a section of the cemetery specifically for Masons, and while the flat bronze grave markers would still have to be employed, allow the Masons to construct a monument of modest dimensions on a 6 foot by 10 foot concrete pad for the entire section, encompassing numerous Masonic symbols that showcased their proud heritage.

The drawing for the monument that Jon was shown before its construction began depicted the front of a small Greek temple that took up half of the pad, consisting of the columns and the frieze of the temple façade. On the portion of the pad behind the temple, three short columns, aligned across the pad and spaced equally, were to be placed. Of the three columns, the one in the center would be the tallest, the other two being the same height. The top of each column displayed a disk embossed with a Masonic symbol. The center column held the Compass and Square. The column to its right featured the All Seeing Eye on top of a pyramid. The last disk, on the other side, displayed the Double Eagle of the Scottish Rite. None of the columns with disks were taller than the top of the frieze of the temple, so that an imaginary line running from top of the disk of the center column to the top of each of the other two disks would be parallel to the top of the frieze. To the front of the Greek temple stood a one foot by four foot rectangular granite marker set at a 60 degree angle that simply read: MASONIC GRAVES.

Jon was surprised how quickly the project came together. There had been very few hitches in the construction, and the monument was completed within a matter of weeks. The craftsmanship was superb, and Jon was seriously considering having other monuments placed throughout the memorial park. That only drawback that he could see was that the "Greek" temple looked more like the front of the Bank of Scotland in Edinburgh – but, go figure.

As the funeral progressed, Jon stood quietly, yet attentively, near the back of the assemblage, to the side of the chairs filled with mourners. Suddenly, from the distance, Jon thought he heard the sound of two cats fighting near the house. There was a wafting quality to the noise due to the inconsistency in the strength of the breeze that was moving across the cemetery, and Jon had to really concentrate on the commotion to determine if it was really two cats locked in combat. He listened intently. It sounded like cats fighting, he thought, but then again, maybe it wasn't. He wondered what could possibly be making that racket.

Just then, an elderly gentleman got up from his chair in the back row and came over to Jon.

"Do ya hear that wailing, Laddie?" The man said with a Scottish brogue.

"To be truthful," Jon answered, "I don't know *what* is making that sound."

"It's a Banshee, Man!" The old man bellowed.

"I've heard the term before, but I don't know if I'm up on the folklore," Jon replied.

"A Banshee, Son! The Wailing Woman! The Harbinger of Death!"

"Well, she's certainly in the right place for it," Jon said in an offhand remark.

"No, Man! Not for poor Jameson, here – he's already gone. This is foretelling someone else's death!"

Jon looked at the old man. His pallor, a shade of gray, clearly suggested that he was already within the grasp of death. But there was a look of terror on his face that was disquieting.

Resuming his role as funeral director, Jon said, "Let me get you a chair."

Walking over to the nearest row of seats, Jon grabbed a vacant folding chair. Going back to the old man and moving him far enough away from the rest of the mourners so as not to disturb the service, Jon unfolded the chair and set it down for the elderly gentleman, gesturing for him to sit down. Once the old man had taken his seat, Jon went down on his haunches, taking hold of the top of the chair back to steady himself.

"Now," he said, "are you all right, Sir?"

The man looked over at Jon with fear yet showing in his eyes.

"But the Banshee," the old fellow exclaimed, almost in a whisper, "she's still coming!"

"Sir . . ." Jon said, trying to think of what he might say to calm the gentleman down. At that moment, Jon noticed that the sound of the cat fight, or whatever it was, was no longer present. He stood up next to the old man's chair.

"Listen to that," Jon said. After a brief pause he added, "Silence!"

The old man strained his ears, searching to detect any trace of the audible dread. Hearing none, he rejoiced, "You're right, Laddie, the wailing is gone!" There was notable relief in the man's face.

Just then, Richie came walking towards his dad. Clad in a kilt and other piper's regalia, a bagpipe slung under his left arm, he thought he might perhaps be able to add a dignified touch to the Scottish Rite funeral. Seeing that the service was still progress and not wishing to disturb, he quietly said to his dad, "Did you hear me playing?"

Jon responded with, "When? Just now?"

"Yep, I just finished."

Jon broke out in a big grin. "You know," he said, "I thought I was hearing two felines having a disagreement!"

"Nope!" Richie said. "It was me."

Jon looked at the elderly gentleman and said, "Well, I think we've found your Banshee."

The old man smiled softly at Richie and said, "So, that was you, Son, wailing like a Banshee?"

Richie looked at his father for clarification.

"The Harbinger of Death," Jon calmly explained.

Turning to the old man Richie finally replied, "I'm not certain about sounding like a Banshee. Someday I'd like to wail like Boots Randolph, but I don't think he plays the pipes. Besides, I need a lot more practice."

"I guess I'm not going to die after all," the old man said with a grin, "at least, not anytime soon!"

"Not for a good long time," Jon offered, to be polite.

"In that case," the elderly gent said to Richie, "you can play at my funeral." With a laugh he added, "But take your time getting better, because I'm not in any hurry!"

Eighteen

The Company's program to dispose of bodies, as one might expect of any good clandestine operation, began under the cloak of darkness. Originally, the processing was scheduled to start at 2 in the morning. But since the local bars all shut down at that hour, it was feared that an inebriated soul might accidentally stumble (both figuratively and literally) across the operation. In their alcoholic stupor they may not have been able to deduce what was actually taking place, but it was decided to push the start time back to 3 A.M. - just to be prudent.

The bodies belonged to foreign government buttinskies that took exception with how we decided that things should be done in their country, and to deal with the problem, The Company had them terminated. Occasionally, assassination would be employed – but the preferred modus operandi for the removal of these annoying persons was usually by kidnapping, and then murder.

Of course, plausible denial was always ramped up in these situations as a smoke screen, but since dangerous repercussions could come from the discovery of the truth, no tangible evidence of the crime could be left behind, which meant that some means of disposing of the bodies would have to be generated. From that need, this plan was devised.

After making their way from overseas in body bags, frequently by way of serendipitous and ingenious modes of transportation for a least a portion of the route (in the sidecar of a Harley, as ballast for a hot air balloon, in the freezer of the QE2), the victims would be assembled at a central distribution point, fed into the tubes of the previously mentioned black decoy trailer, and then set off for the converted weed killer plant to arrive at 3 in the morning for processing.

Then, under the cover of darkness, the pre-embalmed bodies in their body bags were shifted onto gurneys, quietly rolled inside the building, de-bagged, given a spritz bath, and then placed into cheap particleboard caskets (to keep the cost down, of all things!). Innocuous looking white vans, disguised as floral shop delivery vehicles, would be loaded with a casket, and in the obscuration afforded by pre-dawn light, depart unceremoniously for the cemetery.

Early in those morning hours, a crew would already be at work preparing a grave for the burial. The van would drive along the access road and pull up next to the grave site, looking very much as though it was biding its time to deliver flowers. That was the ploy, at least. In actuality, though, the crew was digging a special grave for this van and the others like it – a deeper grave designed to accommodate the cheap casket brought from the processing plant to be placed below the coffin from a legitimate funeral to be held later in the day.

With the extra depth, an additional concrete liner could be lowered into the grave. The particleboard casket would be extracted from the disguised flower shop van (after first verifying that no one was observing the operation), and then, while being slung under the bucket of the front-end loader, would be set in place.

The whole process was quick and as dignified as it had to be for the interment of a bad guy that had been viewed as a threat to our interests overseas. Another concrete liner for the rightful owner of the burial plot, would be placed on top of the one already installed , with the site then being made for the funeral service yet to come. From the outward appearance of the newly prepared grave, no one would be the wiser. The crew members, specially trained ex-military, were sworn to secrecy under the tenants of national security. It was a well-conceived, well carried out operation with very little possibility of discovery.

What has to be understood here is that these victims didn't come from any of the high profile Company murders that made headlines in the paper – Patrice Lumumba in the former Belgium Congo, Rafael Trujillo in the Dominican Republic – it's even suggested that U.N. Secretary General Dag Hammarskjold may have died in a plane crash in Africa engineered by The Company, but that's only speculation. No, the poor individuals destined for the bottom portion of these piggyback graves had no identities. They were minor officials from overseas governments that The Company deemed as being dangerous and required elimination. More often than not, they simply vanished from sight, never to be heard from again. From life, to a body bag, to an unmarked grave in a country that was not their own – it could easily be somebody's worse nightmare come true.

Nineteen

Sitting at the breakfast table with her eyes closed, Ellen June had her feet in a plastic basin, with an ice bag covering her toes. "These bunions are killing me!" Ellen said to the empty kitchen. The treatment with the ice bag did give her some relief, but not enough for her liking. "Thanks a lot, Mom," Ellen June added in sarcastic gratitude to her mother for her gift of bad feet.

Just then, Richie walked into the kitchen to feed his teenage appetite. Seeing his mother sitting alone at the table with her eyes closed, and not being aware of the basin and ice bag located under the table, he couldn't quite understand the expression of minor discomfort she had on her face. Walking up to her he asked, "What's going on, Mom?"

"Quiet suffering, that's what," Ellen June responded, shifting slightly in her chair so that the basin could be seen.

"Oh," Richie said, with the basin now in full view, "bunions again?"

Ellen, with eyes still closed, merely nodded her head in the affirmative

"What are bunions, anyway?" Richie inquired.

"Swelling at the base of the big toe – makes them turn inward," Ellen June answered, almost sounding clinical.

"And you get those how?"

"Usually from ill-fitting shoes, some say, but in my case it was an inheritance from your grandmother. Her bunions were so bad that her big toe could almost shake hands with her little toe."

"OK," Richie said, "that's interesting - and scary. So, how did she get them?"

"Bad shoooooooes!" Ellen June comically responded, getting a laugh out of her son.

Richie then inquired, "Does putting an ice bag on your toes help much?"

Ellen opened her eyes, glanced at the boy and said, "Not really, but it gives me some quiet time to take a load off." With a gentle smirk she added, "Besides, it's a perfect opportunity for me to be able to silently curse your grandmother!"

Smiling at his mother, Richie said, "Well, I'm sorry you're in pain, Mom."

"Thanks, Sweetie," Ellen June responded. Still in a contemplative mood she offered, "They say that suffering is good for the soul."

"And I wonder who might have determined that?" Richie pondered.

"Some poor tortured soul, I suppose," was Ellen's answer.

"Not to change the subject," the hungry lad said, "but what's to eat around here?"

"Well, there's half a sandwich left in the fridge that I made for your dad, with liverwurst and chunks of sharp cedar cheese," Ellen June replied. In an aside she said, "I'm not entirely certain how he can eat that, though."

Richie, easily hearing a comment that wasn't meant for him, said, "It's probably all that mayo he puts on it – he could even make his way through a sandwich made out of road kill with enough of that stuff, I'd bet!"

"As far as I'm concerned," Ellen said, "liverwurst could easily qualify as road kill. But, your dad woofs it down like a vacuum cleaner sucking up dust bunnies."

"Why didn't he finish it?"

"He didn't have time – two funerals today."

"He'll probably want to eat the other half when he's all done," Richie said, "so I'll leave it for him. Anything else?"

"Well, I baked some cookies this morning," Ellen replied. "I put them in the cookie jar on the counter," she added while awkwardly pointing with her left hand over her left shoulder to the container located behind her.

"I better get some of those before grandpa finds out!"

"You're too late – he already knows," Ellen June said, seemingly disgruntled. "I think there are a few left, though, so you might want to grab them before he makes a second run."

Richie walked over to the cookie jar and fished out a cookie. He took a bite as he turned to go over to the refrigerator, and then stopped. Turning back to the container, he took another cookie out of the jar. Holding it up while still chewing his first mouthful of cookie he somehow managed to say, "Just in case he comes back." As he walked past Ellen, his mouth still full of cookie, Richie nevertheless succeeded in asking, "Can I get you anything?" She replied in the negative.

Reaching the fridge, he opened the door and took out an apple. He then walked over to the kitchen table and sat down in a chair across from his mother. Taking alternate bites of the cookie and the apple, Richie, skillfully, was still able to ask Ellen how she and Jon had met.

"Didn't I already tell you about that?" Ellen June said, somewhat surprised.

"No," Richie mumbled with a mouth full of cookie.

"Why are you asking about it now?" Ellen queried.

"I wasn't that curious about it before, I guess," her son replied.

"Well," Ellen said with a chuckle, "it's actually kind of funny. We met at a hog calling contest at the county fair back in Iowa."

"That's certainly romantic," Richie replied in a flippant manner.

"Oh, shut up!" Ellen June playfully, but lovingly, replied. Richie still had a skeptical look on his face. "No, really," she added, "it was romantic - well, sort of – but it was fun."

Richie just rolled his eyes back into his head.

"Well, it was!" Ellen forcefully said. "For a farming community, the county fair was a big deal. It gave everybody a chance to socialize – it was exciting, actually."

"Not much going on out in the sticks, was there?" Richie teased.

"If you put it like that, I suppose not," Ellen June responded, "but that's why the fair was so appealing."

"Wait a minute," Richie suddenly said, "your family was in the funeral business, not farming. So why did you go to the county fair?"

"Because, we served the community – we were a part of it."

"You mean, it was good for business," Richie said, once more kidding his mom.

"We had the only funeral home in town, so people naturally turned to us when there was a death in the family. But these were our friends, as well. When you're dealing with dead people all the time, it's kind of nice to be able to interact once in a while with someone who is breathing."

"Why was Dad there? He lived in a town twenty miles away."

"He liked pigs," Ellen answered, in all seriousness.

"Really?" Richie asked with disbelief.

"That's the truth! I accidentally bumped into him while we were at the pen of this really huge sow and he blurted out, "You know, if you put lipstick on that pig it'd look just like my last blind date, only prettier!"

Richie let out with a laugh and then said, "He didn't!"

"Yes, he actually did."

"What did you say?"

"Nothing. For a while I just stood there looking down, giggling. I finally glanced over at your dad. He broke out in this big grin and winked at me."

"Oh, that's swill!" Richie said.

"You're such a wise acre!" Ellen June replied, with a good natured admonishment.

The young man smiled broadly at his mom.

"I've seen that grin before," Ellen quickly said.

"I wonder where?"

"On a gorilla!" Ellen responded, feigning minor exasperation. She smiled and then rhetorically added, "Where else do you think?"

Richie, choosing to ignore the question, said, "You didn't ask him about his blind date?"

"No, we never got around to that. We just started talking about the pig – how big she was, how many piglets she might have had, what kind of house she lived in to fend off the big, bad wolf . . ."

"Stop the bus!" Richie said, interrupting her explanation. He looked over at Ellen who was now sporting a Cheshire cat grin. Shaking his head, showing he wasn't really buying her spiel, he challenged his mother, adding, "No you didn't!"

"Didn't what?" Ellen June quickly responded, still grinning.

"Talk about the big, bad wolf."

"Ah, but we did," Ellen replied.

"OK – I'm game. Why?"

"Just because your dad and I are naturally silly, I suppose."

"Nothing more than that?"

Ellen hesitated for a moment and then said, "Well, maybe it was the situation. People don't want to seem too serious at a time like that – you know, first impressions and all that, so they say silly things, perhaps as a defense mechanism."

"A defense mechanism against what?"

"Flying pigs dropping bombs! Geez!" Ellen immediately curtly replied, but not actually miffed at her son. Searching for a more suitable answer she said, "I don't really know why. Perhaps it's so the other person doesn't get to know what you're really like. My brother used to say, 'Don't let Ellen out in public, or she'll never be able to get a date' – with that in the back of my mind, I guess humor just seemed like the best way to handle those sweaty palms social situations."

"But you and Dad have always seemed so at ease with each other. And you both *are* naturally funny, too."

"I guess we were just lucky to meet when we did – don't know if it was a match made in heaven, but we're just one of those fortunate couples where everything seems to have clicked from the very beginning."

"So, did Dad ever tell you about his blind date?"

"Yes, he did – years later. He only mentioned to me that the woman looked more like a horse than a pig."

"I didn't know he was so fond of farm animals."

"He's more interested in seeing them on his plate – not horse, at least not that I know of – but pig, yes – bacon, ham steak, baked ham, all things pork!"

"Snout likely to turn down pig's feet, either," Richie said with a grin.

Ellen looked at her offspring for a moment and then said, "I'm trying to remember if we dropped you on your head when you were a baby – that would explain a lot." Richie just sat there, smiling. Ellen June concluded

65

with, "But yes, he even likes pig's feet, which only disgust me, but, to each his own."

"So, when was your first date?" Richie inquired.

"That first meeting actually turned into a date."

"How did that happen?"

"Well, when we were at the pig pen an announcement came over the P.A. that the hog calling contest was about to begin and that everyone was welcomed to give it a shot."

Richie looked at his mom, again with a doubtful eye.

Seeing her son's disbelief, Ellen June simply tilted her head back and shouted, "SOOEEE!"

The boy let out with a laugh and said, "Mom, did grandma drop you on *your* head when you were a baby?"

"More than once!" Ellen replied.

Smiling, Richie asked, "So you did this on a lark?"

"Yep – me and your dad, both."

"Come on – dad too?"

"Why wouldn't he? He has an adventurous spirit. Of course, I was much better – see, I'm taller – more space for my diaphragm – I can really dredge it up! I shut your father down!"

"You bested dad on your first date?"

"You bet I did!"

"Do you think that was wise?"

"Your father was completely all right with it."

"How do you know?"

"Well, he kept bowing to me, saying, 'Salami, salami, bologna!'"

Seeing that his family quirkiness was more extensive than he had originally thought, Richie said, "You guys belong in an asylum!"

"That's so sweet," Ellen responded. "Thank you, Darling."

"It's a left-handed compliment, Mom."

"Thanks just the same, Sweetie."

At that point, Ellen looked down at the basin. "My word," she exclaimed, "my toes must be little blocks of ice by now. Time to take them out!"

Ellen June removed the ice bag and took her feet out of the basin. As she dried them and was putting on her shoes she said, "It's a good thing it's summer, because doing this treatment in the winter is a killer. If I heat up the little guys too quickly after icing them, I get chilblains – and them puppies hurt!"

She picked up the basin with the ice bag and then turned to Richie and said, " I'm going into the bathroom to get rid of this stuff, then I'm going potty. I'll be right back."

Richie waved to his mother as she left the room and then sat quietly for a moment, reflecting on the pachinko like quality of the parental gene pool from which he had been spawned. Being normal, he decided, was overrated, having a slightly bent personality was more interesting. Besides, he mused, when people perceive you as being a little "out there", it gives you a whole latitude of behavior for acting out that you never before even considered. Richie smiled over that thought.

Ellen June came walking back into the kitchen, smiling. "That's much better," she said to her son.

Returning to his parent's first date, Richie asked, "What year did you and dad meet?"

"It was 1945," Ellen said. Thinking momentarily, she then corrected herself and said, "No, it was 1946. Your father didn't come home right after the war ended. He stayed in Europe for a while for the administration of some military matters, at least I think that's what he said."

"Did he ever tell you what he did during the war?" Richie asked.

"No. Your dad just mentioned that he was in the service. He never talks about his war experiences, and I guess that's normal. From what I've heard, though, for most service men, the war was horrible, so I've never pushed him about it."

"Yeah," Richie commented, "he's never told me anything about his time in the service, either. But you're right. Most GIs don't like to talk about being in the war, because people that haven't experienced it can't relate to it. I guess that makes sense."

Suddenly, Ellen June smiled and changed mental gears just like a big rig driver shifting down in a Mack truck. "Ooh! Ooh!" She said. "Guess who I saw today?"

"I haven't the foggiest."

"When I went over to the medical center this morning, I had to use the lady's room. Just when I finished washing my hands, who do you think came sauntering through the restroom door?"

"Still clueless," Richie answered.

"The woman you call, 'Walking without purpose'!'" Ellen said with a big smile.

"Get out of town!"

"No, really! I saw her!"

Richie, with a mischievous grin said, "Did the lights dim when she entered?"

"No," Ellen replied, "but I almost blurted out, 'You're a celebrity in our house!' Then I thought that would be a little hard to explain, so I didn't."

"Good call, Mom. I think you got that one right."

Twenty

"We have a problem here," the caller said in conversation with The Company over the phone. "Actually, a potential problem," they said in clarification. "A local woman, in an intoxicated condition, stood in front of the processing facility at 3:15 in the morning, yelling at the building and shaking her fist, claiming that she knew what was going on inside."

"Do you think your security has been compromised?" The Company rep inquired.

"No, I'm fairly certain it has not. No aspect of the processing is visible from any of the windows of the facility – which, by design, are opaque for protection – and the defused background lighting is purposely dim, as well. From the physical presentation of the facility, I don't think that any element of the operation is detectable. As a further safeguard, as you might remember, the starting time for plant operations was pushed back from 2 to 3 A.M. so that there wouldn't be any chance of discovery by foot traffic coming from the bars in the area right after closing."

"How do you account for the woman, then?"

"Our security camera showed her being pushed out of a moving car onto the sidewalk in front of the facility. She appears to be one of the town's business girls returning from a late night date."

"So, what is your concern?"

"She doesn't know anything about the operation – audio from the security tape confirms that – she thinks we're making sausage in the facility – 'saking mausage' is how she put it in her inebriated state. The concern, though, is that, because her public contact is so extensive - police and politicians included - during the course of casual pillow talk there might be some suspicions raised about what's taking place in that building in the minds of others."

"What do you think should be done?"

"She needs to be relocated, just to be safe," the caller said.

"And terminated?"

"No, nothing that extreme – just make her disappear. With the hours she keeps, it shouldn't be that difficult to snatch her off the street, pump her full of drugs to erase her memory, and transport her elsewhere."

"Any idea where?"

"Fire Island would be ideal – it's a resort area frequented by gay men, and it's not likely she'd be able to ply her trade there."

Twenty One

"Eternal rest grant unto her, O Lord," the priest said while standing before a casket at an open grave.

"And may the perpetual light shine upon her," those attending responded.

Jon was overseeing a service for a young woman in her thirties who had died from breast cancer, leaving behind a loving husband and two small children. Standing slightly off to the side of the last row of folding chairs, Jon was quietly moved by the sustained weeping of the sorrowful gathered while the prayers for the departed continued. These were the deaths that he found so hard to understand – a young mother taken away from her loving family at the time of their greatest need – Jon failed to see how such deaths could possibly serve a purpose in God's plan.

As the service continued, Richie came walking towards his dad from behind, stopping when he reached his father's side. Dressed in a suit, he remained silent while waiting for Jon to acknowledge his presence. Jon, also in business attire, stood solemnly with hands crossed, just below the level of his waist. He eventually peered over at his son and gave a brief, gentle smile.

"I just came in case you needed some help," Richie said to Jon in a low voice.

"Thank you, Son," Jon quietly responded.

At the conclusion of the service, the priest closed his book of prayers and stood somberly for a moment at the grave. Turning, he then walked around the casket to offer his condolences to the husband, children, and the other family members in the front row of seats. Most of the mourners remained seated, talking very little. Gentle weeping still came from the dignified assembly.

With the departure of the priest, the husband, taking the hand of each of his children, walked closer to the grave. After briefly standing before the casket in silence, he released the children from his hold. Leaning over, he lovingly caressed his wife's coffin and then gave a gentle kiss to the smooth, gleaming vessel that contained the mortal remains of his wife. Straightening up, he looked down at each child, took their hand and then slowly turned and walked away from the grave. As he did so, Jon joined the father and his children to escort them to the waiting limousine. Richie made his way towards the front row of mourners to offer any assistance where he could. He remained and talked with the elderly relatives who frequently appeared shocked and disbelieving after the burial of a loved one so much younger than themselves. They always were appreciative of the support they received at such a difficult time. With the elders quiet again and mostly somber, Richie assisted them as they gradually made their way to another waiting family car.

When they were through attending to the family, Jon and Richie stood off to the side, politely and quietly, waiting for the rest of the mourners to depart. Afterwards, they supervised the beginning preparations for the lowering of the casket into the grave until the crew had the task well in hand, and then they left.

"This one was tough," Jon said to his son as they walked away from the grave site. "Father and small children left behind – it's always hard to watch," he added.

Reaching Jon's car, they got in for the drive back to the house.

"I feel for the dad," Richie said as he closed the car door. "I don't know how he's going to manage with two small kids."

"You'd be surprised," Jon replied. "I've seen more than my share of these deaths with the same family dynamics, and it's really amazing how the remaining parent always manages to find the inner strength to carry on."

"Where do you think that comes from?"

"Faith, most certainly," Jon answered. "The thought that death is not the end, but a transition, seems to lessen their pain."

"Do you think it's as simple as that?"

"Well, for some it's definitely a big part of it."

"What about that biker service you directed this morning - probably not the same?"

"They usually aren't. This group was pretty hardcore – didn't believe in either heaven or hell. To them, death is the end of the line and a funeral is just an excuse to have one heck of a party. Giving their fellow biker a big sendoff is the only thing important in their minds."

"Not very traditional, then?"

"Hardly. As I said, this group was hardcore. It broke my heart to see it, but they poured a whole bottle of whiskey onto the casket in a salute to their fallen friend. One guy even tried to pee in the grave to show his contempt for death and the way it took his buddy away. Thankfully, he fell down drunk before he could get his fly completely unzipped."

"That could have been really disgusting!" Richie exclaimed.

"Well," Jon said, "the service did have its repulsive moments, but in a way, there was a certain kind of sincerity and respect that was hard to deny."

"Let me know the next time you have a biker's funeral," Richie said as the car pulled into the driveway. "I'd like to give you a hand with the service."

"It wouldn't be too rowdy for you?" Jon asked in jest, knowing his son was perfectly capable of assisting him with any funeral.

"Actually, I think it would be educational, not to mention entertaining!" Richie responded.

"OK. Next time, you're in!"

"Great!" Richie said, and then quickly added, "But you better not tell mom about it."

After a moment's reflection Jon replied, "You're right, Son - no sense stirring up a hornet's nest!"

Walking to the front door of the house from the car Jon said, "Oh, by the way, I got a request from a family for you to play your bagpipes at the funeral of their father next week."

"Gee, Dad. I don't think I'm ready yet. I'm still not very good."

"I told them that," Jon responded, "but they didn't seem to think that would be a problem."

"That's strange - I wonder why?"

"Because their father was the little old man that thought you were a Banshee."

Twenty Two

Jon sat alone at the kitchen table looking over a letter. "I don't believe this," he said out loud. He was shaking his head and chuckling as he continued to read. "This is really something."

Just then, Samuel Jung walked into the kitchen. "Cookie break!" Jon's father announced when he saw his son sitting at the table. Going over to the counter, he took the top off the cookie jar and pulled out one of his favorites: a chocolate chip Ellen special. "Love these cookies!" Samuel said as he took his first bite. With a look of pleasure spreading over his face, he glanced over at Jon and, while still chewing, asked, "Want one?" Holding up his hand indicating that he already had his quota for the day, Jon declined. "Your loss," the elder Jung said.

After getting his second cookie from the Jar, Samuel walked over to the table and sat down with his son.

"What are you reading?" He asked, before starting on his second cookie.

Jon, completely engrossed in the letter, finally said, "This is incredible."

"Company business?" Samuel inquired.

Putting down the correspondence, Jon looked at his dad and said, "I don't really know."

"What, then?"

Jon asked, "Ever hear of Evita?"

"Who?" Samuel replied.

"Eva Peron – the wife of Juan Peron, the dictator."

"Sure – from Argentina. What about her?"

"The military junta that deposed Peron a few years ago wants to know if we can bury his wife here *for a while!*"

"For a while?" Samuel repeated, sounding perplexed.

"Apparently, she's been moved around a lot."

"The reason being?"

"As a diversionary tactic, it appears."

Quietly thinking, Samuel finished off his second cookie. He then said, "OK, let's see if we can piece this thing together. Didn't she die in the early 1950s?"

"Yes, 1952, to be exact," Jon answered.

"Where else has she been buried?"

"It's a strange story," Jon said, holding up the letter.

"Before you start, let me grab another cookie," Samuel directed while getting off his chair to go to the counter. Returning with his cookie, he sat down and motioned with his hand for his son to begin.

"Eva Peron died from ovarian cancer in 1952," Jon said. "Juan insisted on a public viewing. There was an embalming, but no long term preservation was performed – and she was on display for two weeks."

"I bet she looked really good after that viewing was over," Samuel sardonically offered.

"You only have to imagine," Jon replied. "And," he additionally said, "because of the damage caused by her cancer, a lot of preservation work was going to be required for what was planned for her final interment. Any idea how long that process may have taken?"

"A few days?"

"Not even close," Jon said. "Try again?"

Samuel merely shrugged his shoulders, not wanting to hazard another guess.

"Over a year!" Jon exclaimed. He added, "That's a long time to be putting on makeup, buy they say that she actually looked beautiful."

Samuel sat in silence for a moment with his head down, thinking about why so much effort had been expended in preparing Eva's body for presentation. He finally glanced up at Jon and said, "Like Lenin."

"Yep, they wanted to put her on permanent display just like Comrade Lenin in Moscow."

"Who did the work?"

"The letter didn't say, but it mentioned that it cost over one hundred thousand dollars!"

"Yipes!"

"You said it!"

Following a line of logic out loud Samuel said, "So, she was on display for a while, followed by a long restoration – then the revolution came along, and afterwards all you had was an ex-dictator with a dead wife to show off, but no country to do it in."

"Actually, no dead wife," Jon quickly stated.

"OK – so what's that story?"

"Eva was so popular with the people, mostly the poor of Argentina, that the military junta was afraid that the body of Eva, or 'Evita', as the peasants called her, would be popularly enshrined forever – a symbol of resistance – so the junta kidnapped her body."

"Is this on the level?"

"No! Wait! It gets better. Weirder, too. Here goes: After the military swiped her body, they assigned an officer to set up a burial detail – the problem was, the guy had never done it before. While he was trying to get things moving, he stashed Eva's body in a van and parked it behind a theater.

Somehow, people found out about Evita and started leaving flowers and candles at the scene. He moved the truck to the city waterworks and parked it there – the same thing happened. The guy panicked. Burial was out, he decided – hiding the body was the next best thing. Do you know where?"

"In plain sight on someone's dining room table?" Samuel asked with a smirk.

"That comes later," Jon answered.

"You've *got* to be kidding!"

"No, really – that happened. Try again?"

"I'll never guess," Samuel admitted. "I give," he added.

"He stuffed Evita inside a desk that belonged to a fellow officer!"

"Now, you're pulling my leg."

"No! I'm not! That happened, too!"

"This sounds like a Marx brother's movie – Groucho, not Karl."

"Actually, this plot is funnier – dumber, too."

"Well, the letter also states that, in an effort to create additional deception, the government in place in Argentina started shipping out decoy Evita coffins, with fake Evita bodies, to different Argentinean embassies in Europe – its equivalent of the 'Where's Evita?' shell game."

"The poor woman," Samuel quietly said. Looking over at Jon he asked, "Where is she actually buried now?"

Jon glanced at the letter again. "It looks like Rome, or rather, a town nearby." Reading further, he said, "She's been there since 1957, in a grave marked with an assumed name."

"Why move her now?"

"The old shell game?" Jon suggested. "Keeps them guessing."

"I don't suppose this is a forever move – did the letter say how long they'd like to keep her here?"

"Nope – probably for as long as it keeps the junta happy – then they'll move her again."

"That unfortunate lady will never rest in peace."

"It's probably going to take quite a while," Jon surmised.

"How do you suppose they found out about our operation?"

"A Company man, no doubt, caved-in to temptation."

"The usual?" Samuel supposed.

"Yeah – the promise of a wad of cash, a Latin American honey, and a love shack somewhere."

"Do you think this will hurt us?"

"I don't think so – it's not likely that the regime in Argentina is interested in exposing our operation to the American people or to the people of

Argentina for that matter. They're obviously involved in clandestine operations themselves – so they're not interested in starting a tit for tat thing – besides, they've already shown that they're in need of what we have to offer."

"What about payment?"

Jon looked at the letter again. "Strictly cash – up front – a substantial amount from what I can figure," he said.

"We can certainly use the revenue – bonuses for hush money, that sort of thing."

"Should be useful."

"When do we have to be ready to receive her?"

Searching the notes that he had made earlier, Jon said, "In about three weeks – specifically, the 25th."

Samuel briefly gave some thought to the date and then laid out the plan on how they would accommodate Evita's body. "It's a VIP burial, but obviously there will be no fanfare, no press, certainly no mourners. A single hearse will bring her casket from the airport – because it's a diplomatic flight there won't be any need to deal with customs." He then asked Jon for his input. "I don't suppose you've given any thought to what area might be suitable for her interment?"

But he had, and Jon answered, "How about that section where the women with religious affiliation are buried? You know, when they take vows?"

"You mean, Religious Orders?" Samuel queried.

"Yes, exactly," Jon answered.

"You could have just said nuns."

"Wasn't in the noggin at the time," Jon said with a smile.

Samuel shrugged his shoulders and then went ahead and gave his approval for the location by saying, "I don't see why that area wouldn't work."

"I agree. We don't have many Catholic graves there, and it's not often that we get people walking around in that section – so, it should be fine."

"What about a grave marker? Any names in mind for that?"

"Obviously, we can't use anything close to her real name." Jon said.

"Something simple, then. But what?"

Jon gave some thought to a possible name they could give to the Argentinean icon. "I know," he finally said, "how about Madonna?"

Twenty Three

Ellen June stood at the kitchen counter looking out the window. "My word, what a beautiful day outside," she exclaimed. "Why am I stuck in here baking cookies?"

Suddenly, Sammy stuck his head in the kitchen doorway. He didn't say anything, but he had a look of anticipation on his face.

Ellen had a motherly sixth sense about the comings and goings at her kitchen door. "Not yet, Dad," she said, without even looking in his direction. "I'll let you know when they're ready," she added.

The eagerness was gone from Sammy's face and was now replaced by a look of disappointment. He turned and made a slinking retreat from the kitchen. As he left, Richie came to the doorway. "No cookies!" Sammy grumbled while walking past his grandson.

With the pathways of Richie and his grandfather crossing at the doorway, a rare occurrence took place when Ellen June's radar somehow failed her, for she was completely unaware of her son's presence in the room. Still peering out the window, Ellen started muttering to herself. "I was the first female embalmer in the state, but do you think I'd ever be asked to help out? Huh! Once in a blue moon, maybe, but you know how often that happens! Instead, it's always, 'Have you baked the cookies yet?' Geez! And look how well I got along with The Queen – I have real diplomatic skills – but is anyone interested in me because of that? Hardly! Women built tanks during the war and ferried airplanes, but when it was all over it was, 'Back to the kitchen, ladies!' Now, who wants to make use of our skills?"

Richie, upon hearing his mother's tirade, walked over to Ellen June and took hold of her arm. "Mom? Are you OK?"

His touch startled Ellen and made her jump. Turning towards her son she said, "Oh, hi Darling. I didn't hear you come in." Smiling at Richie, her face brightened.

"Sorry, I didn't mean to spook you," Richie sincerely offered.

"Bad choice of words for around here, Son," Ellen said with a chuckle, "you know, cemetery."

"Sometimes I forget where we live," Richie admitted.

"Me too." Ellen June acknowledged. "Or, at least, I sometimes wish that I could."

"I didn't mean to eavesdrop, but are things really that bad for you?"

"Oh, Hon, I was just spouting off with my semi-annual housewife's lament. Every married woman does it. I love being married to your dad and being your mom. The housework isn't bad if I think about something else

77

while I'm doing it, such as embalming bodies, for instance. I especially like keeping the bathroom tidy for The Queen." Ellen winked as she added, "You never know when she's going to come around!"

"I still don't believe that she came here," Richie said.

Ellen June merely smiled broadly and mouthed the words, "I told you so!"

"It was your shining moment, Mom."

"See! I'm capable of doing other things – like interacting with The Queen. It was almost a perfect moment, except for the cookies!"

"Ah, yes – the cookies," Richie repeated.

Ellen June suddenly looked over at the oven. "OH CRAP!" She said. "The cookies! They're burning!"

Ellen and Richie quickly ran over to the stove. Taking a pot holder, Ellen June opened the oven door. Luckily there wasn't much smoke coming out – a good sign, perhaps. Reaching down, she pulled out the cookie tray and placed it on the top of the stove. Clearing the residual smoke by waving the pot holder, Ellen let out with a sigh of relief.

"They're only burnt around the edges," she said, satisfied that the batch wasn't completely ruined. "Your grandfather will eat them."

"Are you kidding, Mom? Grandpa would still eat them if they were burnt to a crisp with a blowtorch!"

"The man has a cast iron stomach and an insatiable appetite."

"Don't I know it!"

Using her hands to form a makeshift megaphone, Ellen June yelled, "Dad! The cookies are ready."

From the front room came an excited, "Oh, boy!"

Looking at Richie, Ellen said, "You better take one before they're all gone."

"Thanks, but maybe later."

In mocked surprise, Ellen June retorted, "Imagine that! A teenage boy in the kitchen, and he doesn't want anything to eat! Mark this day on your calendar!"

"Besides," Richie responded, "I already had something to eat at Susan's house."

"You just ate, and nothing more?" The mother inquired, not as though it was an inquisition, however.

"We studied."

"Each other?" Ellen asked. Now, it was an inquisition.

"No, Mom," the son said, fighting back. "Economics from a textbook."

Delving deeper to get at the real truth Ellen inquired, "Home economics? Housekeeping? Human reproduction?"

"No! None of that! We only studied about goods, production, income, and wealth."

Softening her tone just a little Ellen said, "You poor boy, how boring."

"Tell me about it," Richie said in response.

Returning once again to her serious quest to verify her suspicions, Ellen asked, "What else went on?"

Richie decided to switch tactics and change the direction of the conversation. "Well, Susan's mother is missing," he said, offhandedly.

Ellen didn't even notice the subtlety of the boy's strategy when she asked, "How could a woman be missing in her own house?"

"No, Mom, you don't understand. Susan's mother went out on a date the other night and didn't come home."

"I thought she did all of her entertaining at her place."

"She usually does, but for this date she agreed to meet the guy in town, and hasn't been seen since."

"She was abducted!" Ellen June said, flat-out.

"What makes you say that?"

"Every time I go to the grocery store, I see newspapers at the checkout counter that have headlines about people being abducted by space aliens, or the government."

"And you believe that stuff?"

"About the space aliens? No. Although my cousin Elwood claims he was abducted by aliens once, but that was only after a cow kicked him in the head when he fell down drunk in the barn."

"So, that leaves the government," Richie reasoned.

"Or criminals that kidnapped her for her money," Ellen countered.

"She doesn't have any."

"Or, maybe she was abducted for a sex slave?"

"Not likely. Susan's mom is pretty good at spotting sickos, and she knows how to avoid them."

"So, that only leaves abduction by the government," Ellen concluded.

"And again, you believe that?" Richie challenged.

"It's in the newspapers all the time."

"I don't think that the tabloids qualify as newspapers, Mom."

"Sure they do! Ellen June said, adamantly. "They wouldn't write about something that wasn't true!"

"But why would the government abduct people?"

"National security?"

"In this town?" Richie asked. "Susan's mother might qualify as a space cadet sometimes, but that's a long way away from being a rocket scientist holding important secrets about ICBMs."

"Well, maybe she just rubbed somebody the wrong way? Ellen suggested.

Richie laughed briefly. "Considering the job description of her present occupation," he said, "that's almost funny."

"It is, isn't it," his mom said with a nervous chuckle, which hinted at her embarrassment. She then added, "Not likely, though, huh?"

"No, she gets along with everyone."

"But then again, what if she was just a general nuisance?" Ellen offered.

"To whom?" Richie inquired.

"Anyone," was Ellen's response. "No pun intended here, but she comes into contact with a lot of people: politicians, businessmen, police, neighbors, cow pokes, even carneys when the carnival is in town – the field is ripe for spying, jealousy, blackmail, grudges, and venereal disease."

"And the government can curb all that by having people abducted?"

"The government utilizing criminals to control wayward citizens – a natural partnership, don't you think?"

"Well, some people would say that the government is full of crooks," Richie offered.

"And where there's an association like that, who'd be better at dealing with dirty laundry?"

"I can see the need for that kind of coalition to be used overseas on the bad guys, but why domestically?"

"Training purposes?" Ellen proposed. "They have to learn the craft somewhere before being shipped out of the country."

Richie looked at his mother with bemused wonderment. He finally asked, "How would you know so much about that kind of thing?"

"I tell you," she said, "those newspaper articles at the grocery store are really informative."

"Is that a fact?" Richie casually, but purposely, questioned. He was skeptical about Ellen's depth of knowledge on the subject, but he figured that she was telling the truth about the source of her information, because considering any other possibility would be just plain ludicrous.

"Absolutely! Those papers have all the facts!" Ellen insisted.

"If you say so," Richie replied. "But assuming that the government is behind many of these abductions, why would it freely admit to its involvement?"

"There's no need to deny it."

"Why not?" Richie asked.

"Well, the government probably feels that such a claim is so fantastic that nobody would believe it anyway, so why not let the truth be published?"

"People believe what they want to believe," Richie mentioned.

"Exactly. The best place to hide the truth is right in front of their eyes."

"So, space alien abductions and those done by the government have virtually the same amount of believability in the public's mind?"

"Looks that way to me." Ellen affirmed.

Richie suddenly became introspective. Momentarily lost in thought, he looked over at his mother and finally said, "Whatever the circumstances are behind her mother's disappearance, Susan is still very upset about it."

"That's understandable, Darling, but in this situation, she has to be prepared for the worst possible news."

"I know," Richie said in agreement. "I cringe every time I pass a Dumpster and wonder if Susan's mom is in there - or when I think I see a body in a ditch along the side of the road while I'm driving in the fading light just after sunset."

"You seem to be a good friend to this girl, Son."

"I am, Mom. And we're not doing anything that would make you ashamed."

Ellen June responded with a simple, "OK."

Twenty Four

"Look at this," Jon said while standing in front of the teletype in the back office.

"What is it?" His dad asked.

"Wait a minute, it's still printing."

Reading the message as the machine continued to type, Jon began to smile broadly. He let out with a laugh and then slapped the top of the teletype in excitement as the message came to an end. Jon engaged the "feed" button to push more paper out of the machine until the entire message was above the teletype's paper cutting bar. He ripped the message from the machine and handed it to his dad.

Samuel read the message leisurely, in its entirety, grinned with some quiet amusement and said, "Imagine that."

Jon, a little more enthusiastic said, "Yes! Imagine! We have a celebrity burial!"

"More like a re-burial, actually."

"Well, of course, but think of it, Dad – James Dean, buried here!"

"Anonymously, though."

"Maybe, maybe not," Jon said as he sat down. That's yet to be determined."

"If the purpose is to avoid drawing attention to the move, though, it should be done anonymously," Samuel said. "When did he originally die?"

"1955. At 24. Car accident. California," Jon rattled off.

"Why is he being moved here?"

"The family is afraid that someone's going to steal his body."

"From his grave in . . . where?" Samuel asked, while trying to glean the information from the print out.

"Indiana," Jon replied.

"All the more reason for an unexceptional burial," Jon's dad noted. He then queried, "What would the motive be for the move?"

"Ransom, no doubt."

Samuel was shaking his head. "You know, if someone stole a body from our family plot, I'd tell them to keep it!"

"Me too," Jon said.

"Chances are this Dean kid wasn't even embalmed for burial because he was so mangled from the accident."

"Even if he had a 'quick and dirty' embalming job, if someone did manage to steal his body, it wouldn't take James Dean very long to become a disgusting mess – if he wasn't that already."

Jon and his dad looked at each other and simultaneously said, "Keep him!"

Samuel skimmed the message again and then asked, "I wonder who contacted Agent Murdock back in Virginia to get in touch with us?"

"I don't know for sure, but I doubt if any general knowledge about our 'special services' is floating around out there."

"Which means that the inquiry probably took some convoluted pathway to get here," Samuel speculated.

"Obviously," Jon stated. "And Murdock is too good an Agent to reveal anything," he added.

"That would definitely be counter to The Company's standard operating procedure," Samuel stipulated.

Jon, with tongue in check, said, "Evidently, that pathway didn't follow a straight line, either. It probably went: a family member knew a guy that had a friend whose uncle's third cousin, twice removed, had an acquaintance whose twin brother played golf with a fellow that was a really good friend of Murdock."

"Yeah, that's probably how it went," Samuel said with a smile.

"All heresy, of course," Jon added.

"Of course."

Extending his hand over to his father, Jon said, "Could I see that teletype again, please?"

"Sure," Samuel said, as he handed the paper over to his son.

Rereading the message, Jon looked for the date that the body was scheduled to arrive. Finding it, he said to Samuel, "Mr. Dean won't be arriving until the 23th – that gives us a little more than a week to do some planning. So, what do you think? Crypt or in-ground burial?"

"Well," Samuel said, "a crypt would be easier – all we have to do is take off the outer slab, remove the sealing plate, and then slide the casket into the vault. For an in-ground burial we'd have to open the grave with the backhoe, set up the vault, put Mr. Dean in place, seal the vault, fill in the grave, and then replace the sod – it's a lot of work."

"I agree," Jon said, "a crypt would be easier – besides, we don't know how long our guest is going to be here – we'd have a quicker egress if he was in a crypt."

"OK. So, a crypt it is," Samuel replied. He then asked, "Are you still considering using his real name?"

"What's wrong with that?"

"Do you think that wise, Son?"

"You know," Jon responded, "sometimes I think you're better off hiding something in plain view."

"That might apply if we're talking about some nondescript inanimate object, but the name of a famous person is something different all together."

"How so?" Jon asked. "A person seeing the crypt might just say, 'Hey, that guy's got the same name as the movie star!"

"And someone else might say, "I thought he was buried in Indiana, but I guess his body is here."

"OK, that sounds like a problem," Jon admitted. He got up from his chair and started pacing back and forth, thinking. Finally, Jon said, "What if we just skewed his birth and death dates a bit?"

"That might still be a problem."

"Why is that?"

"Well," Samuel said, pushing away from the table, "someone viewing the marker at the crypt may not be familiar with the dates, but the name is still there, right in front of their face." Standing next to his chair, Samuel started rubbing the back of his upper thighs.

"Are you alright, Dad?" Jon asked, seeing his father's discomfort.

"I'm OK. I just need to move around a little – my darn legs are sore."

"Why don't we go for a walk?"

"You know, Samuel said, "that sounds like a good idea."

As Jon started leading his dad over to the door he said, "I think you're right – skewing the dates may not be enough."

They stopped just before going outside when Samuel said, "I think I've got a name."

"I'm open to suggestion," Jon responded.

"How about, Dean James?"

Jon thought for a moment as he opened the door, "I like it," he said as they walked out. "It verges on the truth, but doesn't give away the secret. I think you've got a winner, Dad!"

Twenty Five

Richie awoke in the morning with a knot in the pit of his stomach – no doubt the precursor to performance angst looming large ahead of the day's graveside recital. Looking over to the corner of the room from his bed, Richie could see his bagpipes perched in an awkward pose on a chair. Strangely, he conjectured, the only time the pipes didn't look like an ungraceful, tangled mess was when they were being held within the artful grasp of a piper.

Throwing off the covers, he swung his legs over the edge of the bed and sat peering at the drapes that covered the window. Since there was no hint of sunlight trying to make its way past the curtains, Richie knew it was largely an overcast day. Earlier in the morning, the sound of random wind gusts could be heard passing through the leaves of the tree outside his bedroom window, making for a blustery day even though they were still in the midst of summer. Not the best kilt wearing weather, perhaps, but perfectly suited to the gloom and sorrow of a burial service for a frail old man.

Realizing the he couldn't delay any longer, Richie got off the bed and walked over to the dresser. Opening a drawer, he pulled out his kilt and other apparel he'd be wearing for the day. With all the kidding he had endured about what he'd wear under his kilt, Richie did opt for a pair of plaid boxer shorts that closely resembled the kilt in pattern and color – providing a camouflaged effect that would allow him to sidetrack the whole question as to what might be showing beneath the kilt.

He had practiced the bagpipes unfailingly, and although his playing wasn't perfect, Richie believed his performance would be acceptable to the family. At least this time, he hoped, it wouldn't be mistaken for the sound of two combative cats having an altercation. Richie also reasoned that attendance at the burial would be sparse – the family was small, friends not likely, and the weather, dismal – all adding up in his favor. Still, even though he was a teenage boy with a ravenous appetite, he decided to forego breakfast, figuring that projectile vomiting due to nervousness wouldn't, in any way, enhance his performance.

Having dressed quickly, but flawlessly, Richie then picked up the bagpipes and walked out of the bedroom. Stopping briefly in the kitchen, only for a glass of orange juice, he waited for his father to finish his breakfast. Saying goodbye to his mother (who said he looked very Scottish), Richie and Jon walked to the front door and out into the waiting morning. Immediately, a blast of unseasonably cold air almost took Richie's tartan hat off his head.

Luckily, he was able to grab the plaid head covering and keep it in place. Unfortunately, though, there was no way to prevent the same gust of wind from passing between his legs. He was certain that, at that very moment, he was sporting large goose bumps on each of his limbs. Richie prayed that they weren't readily apparent to the unaided eye.

Normally, at moments like this, Jon would cheerfully tease his son. But he would never do it at a time that would clearly embarrass the boy. Jon knew that there might be a level of discomfort involved for Richie in meeting his commitment to help out with the service on this day by playing the bagpipes, and he wanted to let his son know that his efforts were appreciated. As they were walking to the car Jon said, "Thanks for being part of this, today."

Richie responded with, "I'm happy to help out, Dad. He was a nice old man – it's the least I can do."

"Well, I appreciate it, Son. I'm proud of you."

Reaching the car, Richie opened the rear door on the passenger side and placed the bagpipes on the seat. At the same time, Jon moved into the driver's seat and waited for Richie to climb into the adjacent seat up front. When both front doors were closed, Jon started the engine and began driving slowly to the Scottish Rite section of the cemetery.

The grave site had been prepared earlier for the burial, with two short rows of seats to accommodate the few mourners that were expected to attend, but as yet, no cars from the funeral procession had arrived. Jon placed the car along the curb of the memorial park's perimeter road so that the hearse could stop immediately behind his vehicle and be in a perfect position to allow the casket to be carried directly from the rear of the hearse to the grave. The funeral home would be supplying the six pallbearers for the burial detail, since there wouldn't be enough potential candidates in attendance to bear the coffin to its final resting place.

Jon and Richie waited in the car, scanning the perimeter road for the hearse to make its appearance. In the car's quiet interior Jon asked, "Are you nervous, Son?"

"Just a little," Richie replied, glossing over his true state of unease.

Providing some needed assurance Jon merely said, "You'll do fine."

When the hearse finally came into view, the father and son got out of the car. Richie removed the bagpipes from the back seat, and then went to the lawn area slightly to the rear of where the hearse would be stopping. He came to attention at that spot. Jon, in position on the lawn a little further beyond where Richie was standing, waited to escort the family to the grave upon their arrival. Finally, the hearse pulled up along the curb and stopped behind Jon's vehicle.

Richie remained at attention, as best he could, near the rear of the hearse. The bagpipes were something of an armful for him, and grasping them seemed a little unyielding, but he was able to manage. Still, he wondered if the experienced pipers had some magical trick that made it all look so effortless. However, even if a little wrestling with the pipes would be required, Richie felt ready to proceed.

The hearse was eerily quiet and still, and if the sole occupant of the coach was the fellow laying supine in the back, that would be completely understandable. But there were two other gentlemen sitting up front that were very much alive. Upon reflection, it might be thought that the dedicated silence existing on the inside of the hearse was being offered as a sign of respect for the recently departed. Further examination, however, would most likely reveal that the reason for this quiet interlude was not that profound. Instead, in reality, the driver and his assistant were simply waiting for the family to arrive, and were additionally allowing time for the mourners to make their way to the burial site before the casket was removed from the hearse.

When the family car did pull up and come to a stop, Jon stepped over to its back door, and after waiting a few moments for the bereaved to regain their composure, or maybe even to garner some courage, he opened the car door. The mourning party was small. It consisted of only five people: the elderly spouse of the deceased; three adult children (two daughters and a son); and finally, a grandchild – a nine year old boy – the child of the couple's son.

Jon assisted the elderly woman in getting out of the car. Remaining by her side, offering his arm for support, Jon and the widow moved a few steps and watched as the three adult children and the grandchild exited the vehicle. Together, the adults waited as the grandchild went over to stand by his grandmother. Asking the young man to momentarily take the widow's hand for her stability, Jon returned to the car and closed the door.

The procession of mourners slowly moved forward with Jon and the elderly spouse taking the point. The two daughters followed afterwards, with the father and young son bringing up the rear - the dad's hand resting gently on the boy's shoulder. As the group passed Richie's position, one of the daughters, middle-aged to be sure, smiled pleasantly at the teen – the intent being purposely alluringly, but because of the constraints of the situation, it faltered harmlessly as a failed attempt at flirtation. Flattered, none-the-less, Richie returned the smile as an expression of gratitude.

As Jon continued to lead the family to the grave site, a late model blue station wagon, obviously, because of its color, a rental not owned by the funeral home, pulled up behind the other two vehicles and parked. Six men, varying in age from thirty to sixty years old, walked slowly forward towards the hearse, and then gathered around its rear door. The driver of the hearse and his assistant exited the funeral coach and walked to the back of the vehicle. The assistant opened the door to reveal the casket while the driver instructed the group about their duties in the burial detail.

Facing the rear of the hearse, but standing about ten feet away, the driver directed the men to form two lines behind the vehicle. Walking between the men, he then went to the casket, loosened the bracket that secured it in place and began pulling the coffin out of the hearse. As he did so, the driver instructed the men to take hold of the rails that ran along each side of the casket.

Richie, in the meantime, began blowing into the mouthpiece of the bagpipe to inflate the bag. When the six pallbearers had completely extracted the old Scot's coffin from the hearse, Richie was ready to play the pipes. There was a possibility that the first note could be a little tentative – it could sometimes warble a bit – but as Richie applied pressure on the bag to produce the note, it sounded strong and true.

Amazing Grace, the song he had chosen to play on this day, came gently out of the bagpipes – the occasional gust of wind giving a wafting quality to the sound. Concentrating on his playing, Richie was mildly pleased with his performance, which he deemed to be adequate, but still decidedly amateurish. As he turned and faced in the direction of the grave, Richie didn't move forward from the hearse until the pallbearers had wheeled around with the casket and had lined up behind him.

Starting out with a measured pace, the piper and the pallbearers made steady progress towards the Scot's final resting place. As they approached the end of the grave at a right angle, Richie went slightly beyond the burial site. He turned left, went a few paces, and then turned once again to face the family as the pallbearers maneuvered to line up the casket with the open grave. Once in position, the casket was slowly lowered onto the supporting straps that spanned the opening. The six men, taking off their white gloves and laying them on the casket, then then turned and walked to the row of chairs behind the family and sat down. As if on cue, Richie played the last note of the song just as the men were taking their seats.

The service was respectfully religious, somewhat brief (owing to the unseasonably cold weather), and not overly emotional due to the long and happy life that the Scot had lived. The son lovingly eulogized his father as a fine man, a devoted husband, and the best dad that he and his sisters could have possibly hoped for. He told about how his dad, at a previous funeral, had thought that the sound coming from Richie's bagpipes was really a Banshee – a Harbinger of Death. "Considering where we are at this very moment," the son said with a slight chuckle, "Dad might actually have heard a Banshee on that day."

The man then thanked Richie for playing the bagpipes at the service. "Dad was really impressed with the fact that you were learning to play the pipes – he knew the instrument could be difficult to master. He made us promise that we'd have you play at his service, whenever that might be – it was sooner than we expected, as it turns out." The son, caught up in the emotion of grief, stopped for a moment, but then was able to continue. "So, young man, from Dad," he finally said as he extended his hand towards Richie in appreciation, "we say, thank you very much."

Richie waved to the man, and, blushing a little, gave a nod to the rest of the family - and that was it – the service was over. Remaining by the casket, standing at ease as the family members walked past, he shook everyone's hand and accepted their thanks.

The same middle-aged daughter that had smiled at him before, did so again – just as alluringly, but this time with a hint of sadness in her eyes and a look of resignation on her face over the realization that nothing was ever going to come from their brief encounter.

When everyone was gone, Jon came over to Richie to thank him.

"You did a fine job, Son. You can be proud of what you accomplished."

"Thanks, Dad. It was interesting, to say the least."

"Are you still nervous?"

"No, but I could *eat* a cow right now!"

"Got your appetite back?" Jon inquired.

"Like you wouldn't believe!"

"Good thing we don't have to pass any cattle on the way back to the house!"

"I'll settle for a burger in town, just the same!" Richie said.

"I'll drive you there, but you better get out of your skirt first – ah, your kilt. Sorry."

"That's Ok, Dad, I really do need to change anyway. I don't think I could stand another blast of cold air whistling up the old kilt!"

The father smiled at the son.

As they were walking to the car from the burial site, Jon said, "You know, as you were bringing the casket up to the grave, I thought I heard a couple of cats having a fight!"

"Let's just hope you weren't hearing another Banshee!"

"Around here," Jon replied, "you never know!"

Twenty Six

And the deception continued. On a completely random basis (so that no discernible schedule could be detected), the black decoy trailer would be parked curbside in the dead of night, just beyond the left front of the former weed killer plant building. Its special cargo would be off-loaded, taken inside, processed, and then sent out before sunrise in phony flower shop vans to the cemetery for final disposition in holes concealed by the permanence of overlaying legitimate graves.

Creative genius, of the clandestine kind, was employed here. There was no law that couldn't be broken, no moral code that couldn't be circumvented, no promises that couldn't be ignored in the effort to subvert, stifle, or discredit any government, official, or policy that operated contrary to the way that The Company thought that things should be done overseas to support our interests. It was for those that stood in the way, who had to be eliminated, that this process was devised. It was an extreme model of demonstrated efficiency.

The plan had been foolproof. There had been one near penetration of security that occurred early one morning in front of the facility in the darkness of the deserted street. As will be recalled, a local inebriate threatened to expose the operation to the world as a sausage making facility, an erroneous assumption, of course, but the threat came to naught when the intoxicated woman was whisked off the street, had her memory erased, and was then shipped off to the other side of the country to become the darling of the gay community on Fire Island.

But had The Company deluded itself? Glossing over evidence to the contrary, could it continue to believe that in the entire history of government intelligence operations worldwide, mistakes had never been made, secrets hadn't been divulged, accidents had never happened, or that the foolproof hadn't been breached? It was presumed that this operation was safe and would remain that way forever. But could it be reasoned that it would be possible to dangle this deception in front of everyone's eyes in perpetuity, without there ever being the probability of detection? Sure, unsinkable ships don't every sink. Or do they?

Twenty Seven

Ellen June was sitting in the living room darning socks. She had the television on - for background noise - but Ellen wasn't watching it. A product of the Great Depression, she never threw anything away, including socks that had a small hole in the area where the large toe came to rest. She worked ceaselessly to repair the socks with small holes, although she really couldn't tell you why. Ellen, however, did draw the line at trying to make repairs if the hole was big enough to, "drive a truck through it" as Jon liked to say.

Sliding her hand into one of her husband's everyday casual socks, Ellen could easily stick two fingers through the hole. "Well," she said, "this one's dead." Planning to get rid of the sock later, Ellen June put it aside, then thought the better of it and decided, instead, that she might use it as a dust cloth. In the end, she never threw away any of the socks.

As Ellen was holding up another specimen to examine for a pesky hole, Richie came walking through the front door.

"Keeping the world safe from sock holes again, I see," he said.

Ellen June lowered the sock to her lap and said with a chuckle, "You know, I never thought of it quite like that."

"Neither has anyone else, Mom," came her son's sarcastic retort.

"Where did you learn to be such a smart aleck?" Ellen asked, smiling. She then said, "Wait, don't answer that!"

Grinning at his mom as he walked towards the kitchen, Richie said, "I've got something really interesting to tell you, but I have to get some food first. My stomach's growling like a cougar!"

As he entered the kitchen Ellen commanded, "Try not to make anything that will produce crumbs. I just vacuumed in here!"

"Well, so much for toast," Richie responded from the other room.

Raising her voice to be heard, Ellen said, "Thank you!" With her interest piqued she further inquired, "So, what's the big news?"

"Could you wait, *please*?" Richie said in a mock complaint. "Geez! Give a guy a little time, will ya!"

"No hurry," Ellen June replied, again with a smile. "I'll just sit here and talk to these stupid socks some more."

Genuinely busy in the kitchen, Richie said, "Sorry, Mom. What did you say?"

"I said, I'd like to be able to have a real conversation with someone, sometime."

In response Richie said, "OK. We'll get you a parrot!"

91

Ellen threw her arms up into the air and said, "Why do I even bother?"

Having not heard his mother's comment, Richie suggested, "You can always watch television, you know."

"Oh!" Ellen June replied, "I forgot that was on!"

For a minute or two, Ellen tried, without much success, to find a program to watch on television. When Richie came out of the kitchen with a plate of food he said, "Careful, Mom, that stuff will rot your brain!"

With a sour expression on her face, indicating that she really wasn't interested in any of the programs on the tube, Ellen looked at her son and said, "There's nothing but garbage on there! Would you turn it off, please?"

"Sure," Richie said, just as he bit into an apple and held it between his teeth. Balancing the plate with one hand, apple in mouth, he walked over to the television set and turned it off. Afterwards, sitting down in the nearest chair, Richie continued to eat without saying a word.

Ellen June glanced at her quiet son and finally asked, "Well?"

"Oh, yes. The news," he said as he wiped his mouth.

Before he started, though, Ellen said, "Crumbs," indicating by pointing that she wanted him to check around the area where he was sitting.

Looking down for any dropped morsels he said, "Nah, I'm good."

Once again, Ellen June asked, "Well?"

Flat out, Richie said, "Susan's mother is back."

Seemingly surprised, Ellen said, "What?"

Without hesitation Richie replied, "Yeah, she got back yesterday."

"Well, where has she been?"

"Turns out – she was in New York – a place called, Fire Island."

"Never heard of it," Ellen quickly remarked.

"It's a resort area - kind of – mostly gay guys go there."

"A little out of her element, wouldn't you say?"

Richie replied, "She said she actually didn't mind – it was a nice change of scenery."

Ellen June seemed very curious when she asked, "Well, how did she get there?"

"It's strange, but she said she doesn't remember anything about that."

"Well," Ellen offered, "does she recall how she got home?"

"She hitchhiked with a bunch of sailors."

"That must have been one heck of a party!"

"She said the guys were very sweet – they really looked after her."

"Not like any sailors I've known," Ellen said.

"They were just a bunch of homesick kids, Mom," Richie replied. "Susan said her mom was more like a mother to them. They didn't think of her as a prostitute at all."

"Imagine that," Ellen June quipped, "one more hooker with a heart of gold!"

"Well, I believe her."

"Ever think about buying swamp land in Florida?" Ellen suddenly asked.

Richie looked at his mother as if she was one taco short of a combination. Finally, he said, "What are you talking about, Mom?"

Ellen June didn't respond to her son's question right away – she seemed lost in thought – starring into space.

"Swamp land in Florida," he heard her mutter, "that's something to consider."

Just then, Ellen became awkwardly aware that she had been mentally preoccupied for a moment, and maneuvered carefully to right the situation. "So," she finally sputtered, "Susan's mom is all right then?"

Not quite sure what had just happened with his mother, but thinking, perhaps, that it might have been an episode of early dementia, Richie responded with, "Yeah, her mom said she had a lot of fun. She has plenty of new gay friends now. They showed her how to put on makeup, helped to pick out her wardrobe, even showed her how to accessorize. She's really excited about what she learned."

"Well, God save the queens?" Ellen hesitantly said with a slight laugh, apparently hoping to direct attention away from her momentary mental lapse.

Suddenly, a loud laugh came from down the hall. The mother and son looked at each other.

"Oh, no," Ellen June said. "It sounds like your dad is reading 'dumb blonde' jokes, again."

"Oh, good!" Richie responded. "I'll go check it out!"

Twenty Eight

Walking towards his dad's office at the end of the hallway, Richie wondered what could be making him laugh for so long and so loud. Jon did enjoy 'dumb blonde' jokes, but they were just a little jab in the side and didn't sustain the type of laughter that Richie was hearing coming from the office at that moment.

Arriving at the office doorway, Richie knocked. Not hearing any answer, he cautiously opened the door and peered into the room. Jon was sitting at his desk listening to a call over the speaker phone. Richie's grandfather was sitting in a chair next to the desk. Without saying a word, Jon motioned for his son to come into the room. Stepping inside and closing the door, Richie could see his dad wiping tears from his eyes, laughing at the same time.

Not wanting to interrupt the conversation, Richie merely waved hello to his grandfather. Expecting the same type of greeting in return, he was surprised when his grandfather, in a low voice, said, "Hello, Bagpipe Man!"

"Hello, Grandpa," the grandson whispered in reply.

"Fergie's almost finished," Sammy, talking softly, said of the fellow on the phone with Jon.

"Fergie?" Richie asked, whispering again.

"Yeah. Fergie Ferguson. Do you know him?"

"No, not really," Richie replied, still whispering.

Suddenly, indicating that he had been in the room long enough, Sammy said, yet in a low voice, "Well, time for a cookie!"

With the conversation with his grandson over, Sammy Jung got out of his chair and left the room.

Richie looked over at his dad who had just said goodbye to the caller.

"Fergie Ferguson?" Richie asked.

"I think his first name is actually, Stanley," Jon said. "He started calling himself 'Fergie' when he couldn't stand the name 'Stanley' any more, probably at about age nine, I'd guess."

"Strange to have part of your last name as your first name, don't you think?"

"It may not be that common these days with kids named Dustin or Justin, or whatever the heck they're called now," Jon replied. "Ever heard of anyone named 'Tommy Thompson?'"

"Can't say that I have."

"It wasn't such an unusual practice years ago," Jon suggested. "Don Donaldson, John Johnson, Steve Stevenson – pairing first and last names in that way was rather popular."

"I'd like to hear of the first name of the guy with a family name of Tittlemeyer," Richie offered.

Jon laughed and then said, "If he's smart he'll stick with 'Hans', or 'Fritz', or whatever his actual given name happens to be."

"'Titus Tittlemeyer' was more like what I had in mind," Richie said with a grin.

"Sure it was," Jon responded.

"Alright," Richie said, redirecting the conversation, "Who is Fergie Ferguson?"

"I've known Fergie for years – he lives down in Charterville."

"Where's that?" Richie asked.

"It's about four hundred miles south of here."

"Still haven't heard of the place."

"There's probably no reason why you should," Jon said. "It's one of those unremarkable towns located down in the valley."

Still not knowing the whereabouts of the town, Richie said, "I'll take your word for it." He then asked, "How do you know him?"

"Fergie has a funeral home in Charterville."

"So, this has to be one of your humor in death stories," Richie said.

Jon leaned back in his desk chair and let out with a laugh. "Yep," he finally replied, "and it's a good one!"

"OK," Richie said as he sat down. "I'm all ears."

"Well, Fergie has a friend named, Zad Zaderwalski . . ."

Richie interrupted. "I don't believe this. Another two timing, double dipping name taker!"

"Aptly put," Jon responded, chuckling. "I like that."

"He probably had a twin brother named Zod."

"That, I couldn't tell you."

"OK – so what's the story?" Richie asked.

"Well, Zad was a naval aviator – a fighter pilot in the second world war. Sometime in 1946 he and another navy pilot named . . ."

Richie quickly spoke up. "Please, tell me this wasn't another guy with a double name thing."

"Not this time."

"I'm relieved."

Jon continued with the story.

"The other pilot was named Bill Van Amburg. It seems that Zad and Van Amburg were assigned to help with the decommissioning of a naval air station back in Illinois. The two were going through some lockers in a barracks when they found a box with the cremains of an admiral."

"Did he have two similar names also?"

"Actually, I think Fergie said his name was Hugo Bertolucci, or something like that," Jon answered.

"But Hugo fits," Richie quickly added. "It's the kind of highbrow, blue blooded name an admiral should have."

"Yeah, but Bert would have worked, too."

"Let's not even go there," Richie pleaded.

"Alright – so anyway," Jon said as he continued, "the two started asking around the base to see if anyone knew anything about the box of ashes. It turns out that the cremains where supposed to be scattered over one of the nearby Great Lakes."

"Obviously, they weren't. So what happened?"

"Well, there was a procession of blimps flying over the lake, getting ready to dispose of the Admiral's ashes. The officer in charge was issuing orders to a seaman who was standing at the doorway."

"'Wreath!' The officer loudly said to the seaman to be heard above the engine noise."

"'Wreath!' The enlisted man repeated as he was handed the decoration and then threw it out the door."

"'Flowers!' The officer called next."

"'Flowers!' The seaman said before tossing them overboard."

"'Admiral's ashes!' The office shouted in his final order."

"There was no response. The officer looked over at the enlisted man who just shrugged his shoulders. No one had brought the cremains!"

"Someone was going to catch hell for that one!" Richie said.

"You better believe they were!" Jon replied in agreement. Going on, he said, "This was definitely a major screw-up! Apparently, some officer inadvertently left the Admiral's ashes on his desk when they went out to launch the blimps, and hence, the snafu. Trying to hide the evidence of the foul-up, the officer threw the container of cremains into an unassigned locker in the enlisted men's barracks, hoping that everyone would forget about it – which they did until . . ."

"Zad and Van Amburg discovered the box," Richie said in finishing off the sentence for his dad.

"Yep, they did. But now it was their problem. What were they supposed to do with the cremains? Putting their heads together, trying to come up with a solution, the two were suddenly struck by a flash of genius . . ."

"I know this is going to be good!" Richie interjected with anticipation.

"You won't be disappointed," Jon promised, savoring the story he was about to tell. "Here's what happened: The two learned that there was to be

96

an inspection of the facility the next day, which would also include a demonstration of the 'Dilbert Dunker'."

"The what?" Richie inquired.

"The 'Dilbert Dunker'," Jon repeated.

Richie, still lacking comprehension, looked puzzled.

Jon explained. "For some reason a naval aviation cadet was originally referred to affectionately as 'Dilbert' – its namesake, no doubt, being a fellow that had all the flying skills of a clod busting farm boy."

"Part of the training for a cadet involved teaching the student how to get out of an airplane that had 'ditched' at sea and flipped over onto its back. The device used for this training utilized the cockpit section of a navy plane's fuselage that was attached to a sled. The cadet would enter the cockpit from an elevated platform. From that position, the cockpit would be released to rapidly slide down a set of rails that terminated right at the edge of the water in a swimming pool. Abruptly stopping at the end of its run, the cockpit, hinged at the lower front portion of the sled, would flip over, placing the cadet in an inverted position in the water. The cadet's job was to get himself out of the cockpit."

When Jon finished with his explanation, Richie concluded with, "And that's how the 'Dilbert' got dunked!"

Jon merely raised his eyebrows in surprised acknowledgment and nodded his head affirmatively.

"Did any cadets ever die doing this?" Richie asked with a grin.

"No, divers were in the water in case of trouble," Jon flatly replied.

Richie, wondering why his subtle humor had been missed by his dad, said, "So, that's how the 'Dilbert Dunker' works. How does that fit into the story?"

"This is the good part," Jon said. "On the day of the inspection, all of the officers were in their dress uniforms, including hats. As the group was casually standing around the edge of the pool for the demonstration of the 'Dilbert Dunker', Zad and Van Amburg suddenly snapped to attention and saluted when the cockpit went sliding towards the water. All of the other officers were looking at the two, trying to figure out what was going on . . ."

Jon, at this point started to laugh uncontrollably. Without knowing the reason, Richie started to laugh as well. After a moment or two, Jon, in a sputtering effort punctuated with fits of laughter, struggled to continue with the story.

"They put the Admiral's ashes in a container . . . , and attached it to the front of the cockpit . . . , and when it flipped over . . . , the Admiral's ashes were dumped in the pool!"

Richie, still laughing, managed, "So much for being scattered over the Great Lakes."

Jon, with tears coming to his eyes, strained to say, "Under the circumstances, it came as close to fulfilling the Admiral's final wish as anyone could hope!"

Twenty Nine

A moment of cautionary questioning had appeared on the horizon, however. Had the deception actually started to unravel, or did it merely look as though it might? The problem stemmed from the seemingly innocent alignment of two unrelated activities - each, upon examination, shown to lack any moral justification for their existence. The flesh trade emporium run by the mother of Richie's girlfriend being one. The disposal service for the ridding of unwanted bodies, overseen by Richie's father and grandfather, being the other.

How could the indulgence in the pastime offered at that pleasure palace possibly pose a threat to the clandestine operation in the death business? It couldn't, per se, but what naturally occurred in the depths of passion – i.e. people talking – just might. And in that, there could be danger. Tongues wag, suspicions arise, rumors abound. However, the manipulated truth could always be hidden, or disguised, or handled in such a way that exposure would not be likely. There could, nevertheless, be a hazard present in the form of an official no holds barred investigation.

Politicians, although not particularly skilled in running a government, are unquestionably adroit at digging up dirt, unleashing allegations, and subverting by innuendo. Even with only the slightest possibility of discovery, The Company, considered to be something of a sacred cow by many, could be hounded by a stream of questions that would be unending. Although negligible damage might come in the process, the sacred cow could still get grilled. That had to be averted at all cost.

The Company could easily shift into a damage control mode to deal with the situation, and with the vast resources available, it could readily do so. However, it was more geared for the handling of problems on a grander scale, and not those proving to be only as bothersome as flies buzzing around the ear of a bull. The issue, The Company reasoned, could be remedied at the local level. Their personnel were perfectly capable of doing so. Besides, if need be, "plausible denial" could always be employed if things really went south. There was no better method at its disposal to sweep this possibly distasteful quandary under the rug. A phone call was all that was needed to transfer the responsibility.

Thirty

"Mom?" Richie called out as he came into the house through the front door. Not seeing Ellen June in the living room, he walked towards the kitchen. "Mom?" Richie repeated, reaching the doorway. Ellen wasn't there, either. He turned and made his way to the hallway, looking for his mother in the bathroom and her bedroom. She was nowhere to be found.

From the end of the hall, however, Richie did hear voices coming from his father's office. Going to the door he stopped and listened for a while. His dad was using the speakerphone, meaning, apparently, that his grandfather was probably in the office with him. To Richie, the voice on the phone didn't sound natural, appearing, instead, to have been put through a voice synthesizer. The conversation, too, made no sense.

"We suggest curtailing Whiskey Tango Foxtrot for a while," the voice said over the speakerphone.

"For how long?" Jon inquired.

"That is . . . , uncertain," the caller said, sounding as though they were searching for the right word to use. The voice, too, was stiffly mechanical, as if the caller was reading from a script.

"If Whiskey Tango Foxtrot has to be unearthed, who gets dirty?"

"You guys?" The caller sounded hesitant, the response, vague. Paper shuffling could clearly be heard in the background. A moment later the caller corrected the answer to, "Oh . . . the local station." Then, with more paper shuffling evident, the caller, sounding extremely mechanical once again, said, "Watch for flack. Cover your . . . , ah, butts."

Richie assumed this was a business call, but as far as he could tell, it didn't relate to any aspect of the cemetery operation as he knew it. Wanting to find out what the call was all about, Richie opened the door and walked into his dad's office. As soon as Jon saw his son, he said to the caller, "Can you standby for a moment?" He then quickly moved to hit the hold button on the phone.

"Hi, Son," Jon said, not showing any appearance of being rattled.

Richie, looking quite inquisitive, merely waved at his father and his grandfather as he asked, "What's the call about?"

"Oh," Jon responded, "you know – business."

"Cemetery business?"

"Well, remember how I told you that I came across a way to make some extra money?"

"Not really," Richie replied.

"It was a while ago," Jon said, to clarify.

"Still doesn't ring a bell."

"I asked you not to tell your mother . . . ,"

Finally coming to some recognition, Richie responded with, "OK, now I remember."

"The call actually has to do with that, but I can't fill you in just right now."

"I understand," Richie said, figuring that further questioning wouldn't give him a better explanation anyway.

"Is there anything else I can help you with?" Jon inquired.

"Yeah. Do you know where Mom is?"

"Isn't she in the kitchen baking cookies?" Sammy hastily asked.

"No," Richie answered. "I didn't see her there."

"Darn!" Sammy replied, with some genuine disappointment.

Richie didn't say anything, but simply looked over at his father for an answer.

"All she told me this morning was that she was going out to run some errands," Jon offered.

"Oh," was all Richie said.

Jon could tell that something was troubling his boy, so he asked point blank, "What's the matter, Son?"

"Well," Richie said with some hesitation, but then continued, "Susan doesn't know where her mother is."

"Wasn't she shanghaied to the East coast a while back?" Jon inquired.

Over the speakerphone the caller said, "The woman's a trollop! No wonder she disappears so often!"

Hearing the caller's voice, Richie calmly said, "That's Mom."

Amazed at his son's brash statement, especially since the caller was using a voice synthesizer, Jon responded with, "No way!"

"That's her, all right," Richie said, not being surprised at all. "You can tell by the emphasis she puts on the word 'trollop'," he added.

"Ellen?" Jon said to the caller.

"What?" The caller said, sounding frazzled. Finally, from the speakerphone came, "I mean, I'm not Ellen."

Wanting to get to the truth, Richie said, "Come on, Mom. Admit it!"

There was a moment's hesitation, then came, "Oh, horse feathers! You caught me!"

"Ellen!" Jon exclaimed. "What are you doing on this line?"

"Working," Ellen calmly answered.

Jon seemed flabbergasted. "This is a secured line," he said, "who gave you access to it?"

"I don't know," Ellen June confessed. "I just answered an ad in the newspaper and came to this office. Everything was already set up for me."

Jon replied, "You've got to be kidding!"

"No," Ellen answered. "I got bored sitting around the house, and this sounded interesting, so . . . ,"

"Were you asked any questions?" Jon interrupted to inquire.

"No. None. The job didn't require any experience, either."

"Do you know who hired you?"

"Some guy named, Fred, I believe."

"No, I mean . . . ." Jon, at that point, decided not to question Ellen any further."

"Mom?" Richie said to get Ellen June's attention.

"Yes, Dear?"

"Do you know what happened to Susan's mom?"

"No Dear, what?"

In an attempt to clarify the question for his mother, Richie said, "No, Mom. Listen! Do you know where she might be?"

"Why would I know that?"

"Well," Richie said, "it seems you're aware of things that other people just don't have any knowledge about."

"Yeah!" Jon quickly added. "Like the particulars on this woman and her whereabouts!"

"I heard you talking about it while I was on the phone," Ellen calmly offered.

"But, I put you on hold!" Jon insisted.

"I still heard you."

"Must have missed the darn 'hold' button," Jon muttered.

"Finger probably slipped off because of those buttery cookies we've been eating!" Sammy inserted into the conversation.

"Dad!" Ellen and Jon said simultaneously.

Ignoring his grandfather's interruption, Richie said, "Just the same, Mom," "have you heard anything at all about Susan's mom?"

"Not much," Ellen June replied, adding, "just the usual small town rumors."

"Like what?" Richie asked, hoping to hear something tangible.

"Oh," Ellen replied, "that she went to visit a sister in the valley – or that she had another cross country adventure with those sailors – or that she returned to Fire Island to visit some very dear friends."

Jon spoke up and asked, "Did you hear the rumor that they found her body in the weeds by some abandoned railroad tracks in town?"

When Ellen June didn't immediately answer, Richie asked, "Mom? Do you know if there is any credible evidence for that?"

Again, Ellen didn't answer, but Jon said, "I heard that rumor from the local padre while I was in the post office yesterday, but he didn't believe it was true."

Finally, Ellen spoke, wondering, "Where would a priest hear about something like that?"

"The confessional?" Jon conjectured.

"On a visit to the skin parlor?" Their son openly surmised.

"Richie! Really!" Ellen June scolded.

"It happens," Richie said, in his defense.

"*Not* Father Dan!" Ellen insisted.

"At the grocery store buying cookies?" Sammy suggested.

"Dad!" Jon and Ellen said in unison.

After smiling at his grandfather, Richie, in referring to the last bit of gossip said, "Someone suggested that the more unbelievable something appears, the more likely it is to be true."

"Hide the truth right in front of their eyes," Jon said in a very low voice.

Without hearing what his father had just said, Richie asked, "So, none of you know what might have happened to Susan's mother?"

"Why do you think that any of us would?" Jon responded.

"I can't put my finger on it," Richie replied, "but something's going on around here . . . ."

"I just clean house and darn sock," Ellen quickly interjected.

"I just bury dead people," Jon offered, following suit.

"I just eat cookies!" Sammy said with a smile.

There was silence in the room. Richie finally asked his dad, "Will I ever know the real truth?"

Jon looked at Richie and replied, "Our operation is an open book, Son."

Realizing that he wasn't going to learn anything further Richie uttered, "Hmm." Saying nothing more, he walked over to the door, opened it, and then departed.

Jon glanced at his dad and shrugged his shoulders. On the speakerphone, Ellen June asked, "Did Richie just leave?"

"Yes, he did," Jon answered.

"Darn, I wanted to say goodbye."

"He didn't mention where he was going, either," Jon added.

"Hopefully, he'll be there when I come home."

"Most likely," Jon said. Returning to the unfinished business of Ellen's covert phone call, he further asked, "Are you through, now?"

Ellen June, once again misconstruing the meaning behind a direct question, answered, "No, I have a few more errands to run."

Jon, seeing that Ellen didn't understand what he was trying to ascertain, said, "What I meant was, is there nothing more to the message that you were given to read?"

"No," Ellen June responded, "I gave you everything I had. It was all written down. There were even multiple answers to any question you might ask, that's why I probably seemed a little slow at times in answering you."

"And again, you don't know who placed the ad in the paper?"

"Like I said, it was a guy named, Fred."

"Ok," Jon said, without venturing further.

"Someday," Ellen said to her husband, "you'll have to tell me what this is all about."

"Just business," Jon answered. "That's all."

Just as with her son, Ellen June responded simply by uttering, "Hmm!" She ended her call without saying anything further – not even a goodbye.

Jon reached over and turned off the speakerphone. He looked at his father and asked, "Do you buy her story about how she got this job?

"It's inconceivable to me that she could be part of The Company," Samuel said.

"Yeah, I can't see that being the case, either."

"Still, The Company does work in mysterious ways," Samuel said, smiling. He then asked, "Do you think she knows anything about the operation?"

"Well, the message probably seemed pretty vague to her in terms of its substance, so I don't think she really knew the meaning of what she was communicating. But if her claim about how she got the job is legitimate, I don't think we have any reason to worry."

"What about Richie? Do you think he knows anything?"

"I can't really see how he can," Jon answered. "He's never been around for any of the hidden casket interments, and our processing operations at the plant are well cloaked, so . . . ,"

"I get the same impression," Samuel concurred.

"Still," Jon added, "we might need his help in dealing with our problem."

"Can we use him without revealing anything about the operation?"

"That depends on the plan, Dad."

"Do you have one in mind?" Samuel asked.

"I'm working on it, Dad. I'm working on it."

Thirty One

The time had finally come when The Company decided that the disposal of bodies through clandestine operations would have to end. There was no hard evidence that the existence of the shrouded activities had been uncovered, but prudence, a strange bedfellow in covert maneuvering of any sort, rightfully had to be employed, as far as The Company was concerned, to protect the truth from being dug up, so to speak.

Talk had surfaced, as feared, that a congressional committee was gearing up to hold closed door hearings on the matter. But because of The Company's efforts through disinformation, and with the assistance of key members of the congressional committee, all the supposed "facts" to be discussed would be completely based on rumors, lies, and heresy.

As practiced, appearance before a committee by a Company man was an assigned duty. An artful performance combining bombastic oration and understated razzle-dazzle — the resulting spectacle being something worth seeing. Rehearsed under the watchful eye of a Company lawyer, the performer learned how to navigate the fine line between legality and jail time.*

Although overly lengthy hearings were to be avoided, the re-directing or dodging of questions, searching for answers requiring excessive paper shuffling, masterfully demonstrating apparent incompetence through faulty memory, stalling or wasting time — each, in turn, served to drag out the proceedings. In this, The Company knew exactly what it was trying to accomplish: Cause the committee members to become frustrated and bored, thereby calling the purpose of the hearing into question, and as a result, bring the entire process to a grinding halt. The ploy invariably worked.

Not to be outdone, the congressional committee would provide an explanation to the public utilizing doublespeak to postpone further hearings until additional fact finding could be undertaken before the work of the committee would continue. Eventually, with a delay of interminable length, the hearings would become a non-news item no longer worthy of press coverage, the public would forget they had ever existed, the congress would be off the hook, and The Company would have prevented the discovery of the truth. It was a hell of a system.

(The upper echelon of The Company's hierarchy even suggested that, if ever confronted with something of which they actually had no knowledge, the questioned should respond with, "What I don't know is what I don't know.")

Thirty Two

"There's nothing left in the building that doesn't look like the original equipment leftover from when the plant was making weed killer," Jon said to his father.

"No physical evidence at all linking us to the facility?" Samuel Jung asked.

"What little there was, we've taken out."

The father and son were sitting at the kitchen table having coffee. No cookies were in play, though, since they hadn't been baked yet.

"So, what's your plan?" Samuel inquired.

"Fire!" Jon replied, in an unashamed response.

"Industrial accident or arson?"

"Well, since the place has supposedly been abandoned for a number of years, an industrial accident might look a little suspicious, don't you think?"

"Point taken," Samuel replied. He then asked, "Do you have an arsonist in mind that you've used before, or were you planning on utilizing a nut case?"

"Oh, nut case!" Jon responded. "They're much more inventive," he added with a smile.

"But more likely to screw-up," Samuel cautioned.

"That's the thing, Dad. When people learn that a nut case is responsible, they just figure that the fire got started because the guy *is* nuts!"

Samuel Jung smiled at his son and then asked, "Any lead on where you might find a suitable candidate?"

"Not quite yet."

Just then, Richie appeared at the kitchen door. "Well," he said, "if it isn't the chip off the old block and the old block, himself!" Rhetorically, he then asked, "I wonder what that makes me."

"Saw dust?" Sammy responded quickly, yet keenly.

Rich laughed, saying, "Microscopic, no doubt!"

"There's no need to belittle yourself, Son," Jon said, smiling.

"Actually," Richie replied, "I'm shooting for invisible."

"I haven't quite achieved that myself, but I'm working on it," Jon admitted with a chuckle.

Richie grinned at his dad. As he walked to the table to sit down he asked, "What are you two fine gentlemen doing in the kitchen today?"

"Plotting," Jon said, though not seriously, it appeared.

"Isn't that what adults usually do anyway?"

Before Jon could answer, Sammy said, "No cookies!"

"What?" Richie and Jon responded together.

"Ellen forgot!" Sammy said.

"No, Dad, she didn't forget. Ellen just had to go to the store to buy more chocolate chips."

"Goodie! Ellen didn't forget!" Sammy exclaimed.

Jon turned to Richie and said, "He really likes his cookies."

"I think they constitute a major food group in his case," Richie replied, truly believing his assertion.

"You may be right," Jon acknowledged.

Richie looked at his father. "So," he quietly said, "what are you plotting?"

"Oh," Jon said with a wink, "you know – mayhem, revolution – the usual."

"No, really Dad, what are you plotting?"

"Nothing much," Jon said, but went no further.

There was a brief silence in the room, and then Samuel said to his grandson in a strong, mature voice, "We may need your help."

Richie looked over at his grandfather and stared at him for a moment. He finally asked, "Where did you come from?"

"I've been here all along," Samuel Jung responded.

Richie was puzzled. "I don't understand," he said. "If you've always been here, then why the senior citizen buffoon act?"

"Because it suits our purpose," Samuel replied.

Richie was still confused and didn't really know what to say.

After gathering his own thoughts, Jon eventually said, "You were too young to comprehend."

"Comprehend what?" Richie asked, directly.

"What we do for a living," Samuel offered.

"You bury dead people!" Richie exclaimed while looking at his grandfather.

"It's more involved than that," Jon calmly admitted.

Turning towards his dad, Richie said, "You dig a hole and throw a body in it! How much more complicated can it get?"

"We work for the government," Samuel told his grandson.

In his mind Richie was trying to imagine what possible connection there might be between the burying of dead people and the government. He couldn't quite fathom what that was, but he was suddenly filled with dread from the notion of the ominous implication. After his momentary pause to think, Richie asked, "What's the government doing burying dead people?"

"For your own safety, we can't disclose that," Samuel said.

"But, we do need your help, Son," Jon quickly added.

The boy sat quietly for a moment while considering everything that he had just been told. "Let me get this straight," he finally said, "I can't ask *you* any questions, but *you* get to ask me for my help?"

"It's for your own good," Samuel said.

"How so?" Richie quietly asked.

"You just have to trust us on this one," Jon told his son.

"Trust you? Trust the government?" Richie skeptically asked.

"If not us or the government, who else could you trust?" Jon pointedly asked.

After thinking briefly, Richie's measured response was, "No one."

Then Samuel spoke up, trying to calm his grandson's fears. "Richie," he softly said, "would we ever steer you wrong?"

The boy, staring into space for a moment finally said, "I guess not."

Jon, in a further attempt to reassure his son said, "All we want is your help."

After another brief reflective interval, Richie asked, "Considering what you might be doing on behalf of the government, what could I possibly do to help you?"

Jon, without really addressing his son's question, replied, "Do you know any kids that are a little wacko?"

"A loose cannon?" Samuel quickly offered.

"A sociopath?" Jon added.

"A pyromaniac?" Samuel concluded.

"Well," Richie responded, "I know a guy that is pretty out there. He's trying to find someone who will take him to the dessert in Arizona so he can jump from a moving pickup truck into a cactus."

"Are you serious?" Jon asked, finding such an act of stupidity to be incredulous.

"That's what I heard," Richie replied.

"Well," Jon said, "that fellow obviously doesn't have a lick of sense."

Shaking his head in disbelief, Samuel said, "We're doomed as a species!"

"I couldn't agree more," Jon concurred. "Still," he added, "this could be our man."

"If he likes to set fires, he's a readymade patsy," Samuel said.

"Does he?" Jon pointedly asked his son.

"I don't know for sure, but I can ask around," Richie replied. As a further thought he added, "Are you planning to burn down a building?"

Before either Jon or his father could answer, Ellen June came walking through the backdoor, carrying a grocery bag.

"Chocolate chips?" Sammy excitedly asked as Ellen stepped to the counter.

"Yes, Dad. I bought chocolate chips."

"Oh boy! She'll bake Cookies!"

In response, Ellen June said, "I'll make them as soon as I can."

Happily, Sammy inquired, "Can I lick the bowl?"

"Of course, Dad," Ellen replied.

As she was reaching into the shopping bag, Ellen said, "Lots of excitement downtown today, boys."

"Oh, really," Jon said. "What's happening?"

"There's a fire," Ellen June replied.

"A fire?" Jon repeated for verification. "What's burning?"

"You can see the smoke from the window," Ellen answered.

Jon, his dad, and Richie all went over to the kitchen sink to look out the window. Spying the smoke, Jon said in a low voice, "It looks like it's coming from the east end of town." He then again asked Ellen, "What's burning?"

Ellen June simply replied, "The old Weed-B-Gone plant."

Thirty Three

A couple of days later, on a warm Saturday afternoon, Jon, his dad, and Richie were sitting in the living room inattentively watching the week's televised major league baseball game. With two east coast teams playing, there was little interest in the outcome of the game. The audio from the TV served primarily as background noise for the three as they talked over the events in the town from the past few days.

"Any word on who might have set the fire?" Jon asked his son.

"I've tried to find out," Richie said, "but no one I've talked to will fess up to anything."

"Here's the three, two pitch . . . ," came the announcer's voice from the television set, *"Miller swings and sends a foul ball into the seats down the left field line."*

"Do you think money will buy any answers?" Samuel asked the boy.

"These guys would probably say anything for the money, but what they tell you may not be anywhere near the truth," Richie responded.

"We always have to consider that," Jon said, "but do you have any leads at all?"

The action from the baseball game continued. *"This has been a good at bat for Miller,"* the announcer said. *"He's taken ten pitches from Wilson, who is probably wondering how much longer this guy can last."*

While watching the batter hit another foul ball, Richie answered, "Well, I don't know what this is worth, but I talked with a kid who said there was a rumor floating around that the person that started the fire was aided by a middle-aged woman."

"A middle-aged woman?" Samuel repeated, just to make sure that he had heard correctly.

"Yeah, middle-aged," Richie answered.

"Did he know who she was?" Jon queried.

"I'm not sure," Richie said, "but what's strange is that, out of the blue, she asked the kid that supposedly started the fire if he'd like a box of matches and some fire crackers."

"Wilson sets and delivers," the announcer droned. *"Miller swings and finally misses, bringing the ball game to an end."*

"A middle-aged woman offering firecrackers. Doesn't that seem a little out of character for a female of her maturity?" Samuel wondered.

As the announcer was wrapping up the game, Jon pointed to the TV and said to Richie, "Off, please."

"You know," Richie responded somewhat irritated, "I think the only reason why people have kids is to change channels on the television set or to turn it off!"

"The secret's out!" Jon exclaimed.

"You just wait," Richie said to his dad as he got up to turn off the TV, "one day they'll have a device that will allow you to do all that without leaving your chair!"

"That might be," Jon replied, "but until they do, people will still have kids to handle the task."

Returning their discussion to the fire at the old Weed-B-Gone plant, Samuel again questioned, "Why would a middle-aged woman have firecrackers?"

"And where would she be getting them, anyway? I'm pretty sure firecrackers are illegal!" Jon stated.

Without having an answer for his father or grandfather, Richie added one more item to the mix. "There's something odd here, too," he said. "The guy mentioned that the woman was carrying the firecrackers and matches in a large grocery bag hidden under packages of chocolate chips."

Jon and Samuel looked at each other and simultaneously asked, "Ellen June?"

Richie, upon reflection, said, "You know, I think it is Mom."

"What?!" Jon and Samuel said, together.

"It makes sense," Richie answered.

"What are your suspicions?" Jon inquired, not wanting to reveal what he himself had suspected about Ellen.

"Look at that phone call the other day," Richie said. "Do you think the government would be dumb enough to hire someone off the street to handle a supposedly sensitive matter?"

"Whatever it was," Samuel interjected.

"Yeah," Richie hesitantly responded while looking at his grandfather and repeated, "whatever it was."

"Perhaps, though, it happened exactly as she described," Jon offered.

"And you buy that?" Richie asked.

"It's not that farfetched," Jon replied. "Run an ad in the newspaper to attract a bored housewife who might be looking for a little excitement, keep everything vague so as to not arouse curiosity – that actually seems completely plausible."

"Or," Richie countered, "her story was in fact a smoke screen and she really has some connection to a government intelligence agency."

Looking at his father for a moment, and then turning back to his son, Jon finally said, "Your mother? The one that makes pickled watermelon rind and bakes cookies? What possible proof could you have that she is part and parcel to *any* aspect of *any* government intelligence operation?"

"Because she knows too much," Richie responded.

Treading light, Jon queried, "About what, for instance?"

"About things that a housewife that pickles watermelon rind and bakes cookies would never have a reason to know."

"Again, what? Please tell me," Jon insisted.

"Well," Richie began, "she was able to give possible motives for why Susan's mother might have been abducted by the government - although she also threw in that space aliens may have been the culprits, but she might have done that just to make her look harebrained."

"So what?" Jon challenged.

Richie responded, "She implied that organized crime was used by the government in both domestic and overseas operations, although she claimed she obtained that information from the tabloids at the grocery store."

"That was most likely her source," Jon quickly offered.

Richie, not disputing his father on the point, continued, "She also suggested, for some reason, that swamp land in Florida might be useful, though she didn't say for what."

"She's never been to Florida!" Jon asserted.

"Well," the boy said, "Mom also said that sometimes the best place to hide the truth is right in plain sight."

Jon had no reply.

At that point, Samuel, who had remained silent during the exchange between the two looked at Jon and said, "You know, Richie just might be right about Ellen."

Jon, who was doubtful, replied, "Isn't that a little hard to swallow?"

"Why don't we ask Ellen?" Samuel replied.

Thirty Four

The Company, from early on, recognized the importance of having checks and balances incorporated into its operation. This was done at all levels of the organization, from top to bottom – someone was always looking over someone else's shoulder.

This system of quasi-accountability was undeniably informal. Many of the personnel initially chosen to be in-place tattletales were selected almost at random by way of a personal ad in the newspaper. Ellen June, on the other hand, through her relationship to Jon and his father, was already known to The Company. She had been specifically targeted for her role by way of an anonymous invitation summonsing her to join a bogus neighborhood watch group to promote civic pride by keeping tabs on whatever was going on in her town. Who Ellen was supposed to watch, and what she was to be looking for, was purposely left vague, making virtually all the activities of any person or any organization on her radar truly open to suspicion.

It was reasoned that the most important prerequisite for a successful candidate for this assignment would be that the person have an inquisitive mind. At the same time, however, it was deemed that they should also not be very good at connecting the dots. Ellen June, it was felt, was well suited in both areas for the task.

But The Company had sorely underestimated Ellen's capabilities. She was more resourceful than she let on, and was fiercely more loyal to her family and more protective than was deemed possible. Ellen June was first recruited not long after they had started living on the cemetery. From that time forward, she began reporting back to The Company, but only on the things that she thought it should know about. Other matters that Ellen felt were none of The Company's business were kept to herself. She clearly was not the confidant that The Company had wrongfully thought she would be, or expected that she would likely become. In reality, Ellen June Jung was a rogue.

Thirty Five

The day after the decision had been made to confront Ellen June, Jon Jung stood looking out the picture window in the living room, waiting for Ellen to return from her morning errands. His father and son were waiting, too, curious as to what might be discovered. Just before 11 A.M. her car pulled into the driveway.

"She's here!" Jon said as he watched Ellen get out of the car and start walking towards the porch.

As soon as Ellen June came through the front door, he went over to greet her. "Get everything done?" Jon asked as he gave her a peck on the check.

"Almost," Ellen said, sounding a little disgruntled.

"Oh?" Jon responded.

"Because someone ate all the cookies," Ellen said sharply while glaring at Sammy, "I had to go to the store for more chocolate chips, and then I forgot to buy them!"

"Don't you hate when that happens?" Jon sympathized.

Coming over to Ellen from the couch, Sammy, looking disappointed, said, "No cookies?"

"I'll bake them in just a bit, Dad," Ellen June said as she set down her grocery bag on the nearby coffee table. "They'll only have raisins in them, though, instead of chocolate chips."

"Raisin cookies! Yummy!" Sammy said with delight.

"Hi, Mom!" Richie said as he came over to his mother from his chair.

"My word," Ellen said. "What a welcome! And from all three boys! What did I do to deserve such royal treatment?"

"We're just glad to have you home," Jon offered.

Being suspicious of such a warm greeting upon her homecoming, however, Ellen June said, "OK – what do you want?"

"Only a little of your time," Jon said with a gentle smile.

Intrigued, Ellen said, "Sounds interesting, but you'll have to give me a moment. I've had to tinkle for the past twenty minutes and if I don't get into the bathroom right now, I'm going to have an accident right here on the rug!"

Jon, bowing at the waist, extended his arm in the direction of the bathroom and said, "My Lady, the convenience awaits!"

"Thanks!" Ellen exclaimed as she dashed down the hallway.

When they heard the bathroom door close, Samuel said to Jon in a low voice, "You take the lead when she comes back."

Jon nodded his head and said, "Right."

114

It seemed to take Ellen an inordinate amount of time to "answer the call of nature" as Jon was fond of saying. Her extended stint in the bathroom, however, had come from her decision to stay and clean it up a bit. After perhaps ten minutes, Ellen June came walking into the living room carrying some old magazines in one hand and a bag of trash from the wastebasket in the other. Approaching Richie, she winked and said, "We better keep it tidy, because you never know when The Queen is going to drop by!"

Looking at his mother Richie said, "I've been meaning to ask you – I know I wasn't there for The Queen's first visit, but how did you manage to pull that off last time?"

"Easy," Ellen replied, "I used mental telepathy!"

Skeptically, Richie said, "Sure, right."

Ellen merely smiled.

"OK," Jon finally said, "this won't take long. He grabbed the bag of trash and magazines from Ellen's hands and placed them under the coffee table.

"Cookies!" Sammy impatiently said.

"In a minute, Dad," Ellen June calmly responded.

"Why don't you sit down on the couch?" Jon said to Ellen.

Smiling, as she took her seat, she said, "Oh! Look at this! I've been elevated to a padded throne!"

With Ellen seated, the three men sat down.

"Comfy, then?" Jon asked his wife.

"Comfy!"

"Much better than that hard old chair from the dining room that you usually sit on, correct?" Jon asked.

"Much!" Ellen agreed.

"Well, then . . . ," Jon said with a stammer, "and I'm asking only out of curiosity . . . , but . . . , do you happen to remember if you were anywhere near the old Weed-B-Gone plant last week?"

"Can't say," was all that came from Ellen June.

"Can't say if you remember, or can't say if you were near the plant?" Jon asked for clarification.

"Both," Ellen responded.

"Both," Jon muttered under his breath.

"Plausible denial!" Samuel whispered to Richie so that Ellen wouldn't hear.

"So, you don't remember at all?" Jon again asked his wife.

"Well," Ellen June answered, "I *drive* by there all the time."

"Did you drive by there the day of the fire?" Jon inquired.

"Don't remember," Ellen replied.

"Dodging!" Samuel whispered to his grandson.

"Well," Jon said, somewhat frustrated, "supposing that you did drive by there on the day of the fire. Were there any young fellows around Richie's age hanging about?"

"There may have been," Ellen June said.

"You don't know for sure?" Jon asked directly.

"Not certain," was her response.

"Stonewalling!" Samuel again whispered, giving his take on Ellen's reply to Richie.

At that moment, the doorbell rang at the front door.

They were all momentarily startled by the intrusion, because no one was expected, supposedly.

"I wonder who that could be," Ellen said.

Jon looked at his son as he pointed to the door and said, "Do you mind?"

"Would it make any difference if I did?" Richie grumbled while getting off his chair. Going to the door, the boy took hold of the doorknob, turned it, and opened the door. A woman in her mid-forties, wearing a trim fitting red flight suit and an oversized pair of aviator sunglasses, stood on the porch, smiling broadly.

"I'm sorry to bother you," the woman said with a very proper English accent, "but is Ellen home?"

Richie, trying to place the woman, bluntly asked, "Does my mother know you?"

Unperturbed, the woman said, "Just tell her it's Elizabeth from England."

Jon, upon hearing the voice but not seeing who it belonged to, blurted out, "The Queen?"

"You're kidding?" Richie said as he glanced over at his dad.

Samuel stepped to the door and opened it as wide as it would go, revealing the woman to everyone in the room. Bowing his head he said, "Your Grace! Please, come in."

Once again, Richie said, "You're kidding? Right?"

As The Queen stepped over the threshold, Ellen June came forward.

"Your Grace," she said. Just as with The Queen's first visit, Ellen attempted her awkward curtsy. Failing that, Ellen uttered, "Oh my juniper berries," and promptly fainted to the floor.

"Not again!" The Queen said with a slight chuckle, adding, "The poor dear."

Samuel ushered Her Majesty into the living room as Jon directed his son to the bathroom to get a wet washcloth for his mom. When Richie started down the hallway, Jon turned to The Queen, bowed, and then offered his hand, saying, "Your Grace! Welcome!" The Queen extended her hand and said, "It's been a long time, hasn't it, Jon?"

"Since right after the war ended, I believe," Jon said with a warm smile.

"And you and your dad are still working together?" Elizabeth asked.

"Well, Dad's semi-retired, so we're primarily involved with contract work with the government – you know - special projects."

"I've heard," Elizabeth acknowledged.

Jon, somewhat astonished, inquired, "Could I ask from whom?"

"She can't tell you that," Samuel suddenly said to his son.

"Sorry," The Queen said to Jon. "Security, and all that," she added.

Ellen, from her supine position on the floor, unexpectedly said, "I know who told her!"

Jon, Samuel, and The Queen looked at the woman with surprise.

With her eyes still closed, Ellen June giggled and said, "It was the Easter Bunny!"

The Queen smiled briefly and said, "She must be coming around."

While Jon and his dad were standing near Ellen's feet, the monarch, situated near Ellen June's midsection, knelt down on one knee, blocking the men's view of the upper torso and head of Jon's wife. Bending over slightly, The Queen reached down and touched Ellen's forearm. Ellen opened her eyes, winked at Her Majesty, and then closed them again. Taking the woman's hand and patting it lightly, The Queen turned to Jon and Samuel and said, "Yes, she's coming around."

Richie quietly walked into the living room, went over to The Queen, and handed the damp washcloth to her.

"Will this do, Ma'am?

The monarch looked up and took the wet cloth. "That's fine, Dear," she said. Then glancing over at Jon she added, "Such a nice young man. Do you think he'd like to meet my daughter?"

"If he's smart!" Jon replied with a smile.

"Good. I'll ask Anne," The Queen responded.

Taking the wet wash cloth and applying it to the back of Ellen's neck, the monarch began to coax the woman out of her artfully feigned state of unconsciousness. "Come on, Ellen Dear," The Queen softly said, "time to wake up." Mindful not to say anything that might make Ellen giggle and give away the pretense, Her Royal Highness continued to encourage Ellen to awaken. "OK, Dear. Open those eyes." And as if by a miracle, rather than a command, they did open!"

"Your Grace?" Ellen June queried, managing to sound somewhat groggy. "What are you doing here?" Ellen began to sit up, assisted by the monarch.

"Slowly, Dear, slowly," The Queen cautioned.

It was only then that Ellen noticed The Queen's attire.

"What are you wearing, Your Grace?"

"Oh!" The Queen said, "It's a flight suit of the Red Arrows, the Royal Air Force flight demonstration team. Do you like it?"

"Yes, very much," Ellen replied. "It's so chic!"

"I had it tailored," The Queen said. "The standard issue flight suit made me look like an oversized pear in a red sack!"

Ellen chuckled a bit as she came to her feet. Looking at the monarch she then said, "It's very nice, but why are you wearing it?"

"The RAF needed someone to pass out information pamphlets for the Red Arrows during its American tour and asked me if I'd like to come along. Well, I was getting bored just sitting around the Royal dog house all day long," at this point The Queen reached over and touched Ellen's forearm saying, "you know, the Corgis think the palace belongs to them! They're probably right! Anyway, when I was offered the opportunity, I jumped at the chance to go!"

"Your Grace," Jon said, "aren't you afraid that someone will recognize you?"

The monarch looked over at Jon, smiled, and said, "The English Queen, in America, wearing a red tailored flight suit and a pair of large aviator sunglasses, passing out pamphlets for the RAF's Red Arrows? Wouldn't anyone who might possibly suspect it was me, in the end, think that to be an utterly preposterous notion?"

"Well," Jon responded, "I suppose you're right."

Smiling, The Queen remarked, "That's exactly why I decided that I would do this!"

Jon, returned the smile, bowed and said, "Of course, Your Grace."

"Sometimes the best place to hide the truth is right in plain sight," Elizabeth, Queen of England, offered.

Jon, without saying a word, looked at his father with an expression of minor amazement.

"Oh!" Ellen suddenly said, "Your Grace! I'm a terrible hostess. I didn't even offer you coffee!"

"That' all right, Dear," The Queen responded, "though I am dying for a cup of tea!"

Ellen June motioned The Queen over to the sofa and said, "Please! Why don't you sit here while I go to the kitchen and put on the kettle."

"I should say not!" Elizabeth exclaimed. "I never get a chance to make tea at home. The servants wouldn't hear of it! Let me come to the kitchen and show you how to make a proper cup of tea! This will be fun!"

"Certainly, Your Grace," Ellen June replied.

The monarch intertwined her arm with Ellen's, and before setting off for the kitchen, looked back at Jon, Samuel, and Richie, nodded her head, and said, "Gentlemen."

When the two women had disappeared into the kitchen, Jon turned to Samuel, and whispering, asked, "The Queen's an agent?"

Jon's dad brought the index finger of his right hand to his lips, and went, "Shhh."

Thirty Six

In the kitchen, The Queen turned to Ellen and said, "Dear, this is your home, I wouldn't presume to tell you how to make a cup of tea. Still . . . ,"

Ellen cautiously, yet courteously, replied, "Your Majesty, I would be honored if you'd show me how to make tea."

So, Elizabeth, Queen of England, began to gently instruct Ellen June, American commoner, in the English way to properly make a cup of tea. After explaining and demonstrating each step in the process of brewing the tea, The Queen set the kettle on the stove to heat.

"While we're waiting," Elizabeth said, "why don't we have a little sit down and chat."

As they were taking their places at the kitchen table, Sammy stuck his head in the doorway and asked, "Cookies?"

"Not now, Dad," Ellen said, "but soon. OK?"

"OK," Sammy said, then turned and went back into the living room.

The Queen watched Sammy leave and then looked at Ellen. "You're aware that he's putting on an act for you?" Elizabeth asked.

"Yes, I know," Ellen June responded. "It's predictable and harmless, so I go along with it because it's fun."

"Have you ever seen the real Samuel Jung?"

"Perhaps I did for a while, after Jon and I were first married. But as Dad started aging, he felt the need to take on this second childhood persona, and I let him. I don't even think of it as an act anymore."

The Queen of England went over to the stove to tend to the kettle. She filled the tea cups and brought them over to the table.

"Do Jon and Samuel have any inkling that you're keeping tabs on them?" The Queen asked as she set the cups down.

"They might suspect," Ellen replied as she reached for her teacup, "but I don't think they can envision how a 'lowly' housewife could possibly be working for The Company."

"I get the same thing with my husband," the monarch stated. "He thinks, 'The Queen working for MI5? That's impossible!'"

They looked at each other and giggled.

"Fooled them!" Ellen June finally said.

"Fooled them!" The Queen echoed.

But had they?

Thirty Seven

While Ellen and The Queen were in the kitchen, Ellen's son went outside to look at the red sports car that was parked in front of the house. "Oh, wow!" Richie exclaimed as he walked around the vehicle to study its lines. Low and sleek, foreign and sexy, powerful and fast – just sitting on the street it already looked as though it was going over one hundred miles per hour. Going back to the house, he looked over his shoulder at the car and muttered, "Someday!"

As Richie came through the front door, Jon said, "Some car, huh?"

"You betcha!" The young man responded.

"It's fast, too!" The monarch said as she walked into the living room.

Richie turned to look at The Queen.

"You drove this car?" He asked in disbelief.

"Indeed I did!" The Queen replied. "Do you doubt that I can?" She asked.

"Sorry, Ma'am," Richie said, stammering a bit as he addressed The Queen, "it's just that this car doesn't seem to fit your image."

"I'm not a dowager queen, not yet, anyway!" Elizabeth responded.

"No, Ma'am," Richie politely replied.

"During the war, I drove trucks in the motor pool!"

"Yes, Ma'am."

"So, I know how to drive a stick shift."

"Yes, Ma'am," Richie again said.

"Driving this sports car was a kick!" The Queen gushed, and then added, "The thing can really scoot!"

The young man didn't reply, he merely nodded his head to indicate that he believed the monarch.

"Before I even got off the base, I had already lost the military escort!"

"Yes, Ma'am," Richie once again said.

At that moment there was a knock at the front door.

"Now what?" Jon quietly grumbled from his easy chair. Looking at Richie, he pointed to the door and said, "Please."

"If it's not the TV, it's the door!" Richie muttered as he went to see who had knocked.

Quickly opening the door, displaying some of the irritation he felt over his father's request, Richie was at once taken aback by the sight of a uniformed Highway Patrol officer standing on the front porch.

"Hello, Son," the officer said in a friendly manner.

"Hello, Sir," Richie replied.

"It that your car?" The patrolman asked as he pointed to the red sports car parked out front.

"Sadly, no, Sir," Richie responded.

"I know what you mean," the officer said with a grin. He then asked, "Do you know who does own it?"

Not quite knowing how to explain about The Queen, Richie said, "It belongs to a lady friend of my mother."

"Is she here?" The patrolman inquired without delay.

"Yes, she it," Richie answered.

The officer then patiently asked, "Could you have her come to the door?"

"Sure thing," the young man said. As he turned to call to The Queen, Richie was startled to see that the monarch had already come closer to the door and was actually standing right behind him.

"Oh! Here she is!" Richie said as he open his hands and moved them towards The Queen, in effect, presenting her to the patrolman.

"Ma'am," the lawman said in greeting.

"Officer," The Queen responded.

"Is this your car?"

"Actually, it belongs to Captain Eric Shillings, the commander of Black Rock airbase. He loaned it to me."

The officer looked directly at the woman and calmly said, "Commander Shillings says that you stole the vehicle."

The Queen, at first, looked shocked. But then, remembering who she was, asserted herself. "No officer! He loaned it to me!" Elizabeth insisted.

The patrolman remained poised as he further explained, "I was informed that you were given the car only to be driven on base, and you left."

"No!" The Queen said in a heated reply. "The car was loaned to me to go wherever I wanted to go!"

Still unperturbed, realizing the exchange was now at an impasse, the officer said, "I need to see some identification, Ma'am."

Now, this was a problem for The Queen, because she didn't have any identification — none whatsoever - she never needed it to prove who she was. She did need it at this very moment, however.

"Sorry, Officer," she said, having regained her composure, "I don't seem to have any identification."

The patrolman looked at the monarch for a moment and then said, "None at all?"

Quietly, The Queen reiterated, "I've never needed it before."

The officer remained silent, waiting for an explanation.

"Look," Her Majesty finally said, "I didn't want to reveal this, but I'm Elizabeth, Queen of England."

The lawman, unimpressed, said, "The base commander said that you were from Texas."

"I used a Texas drawl as a disguise while I was on tour with the RAF," the monarch quickly said, showing some exasperation. "It's fairly close to my own accent and isn't that difficult to do. My hope was to keep people at the air shows from discovering that I was actually The Queen. I never thought it would come back to bite me in the butt."

The law officer looked at The Queen for a few seconds in silence.

"So," he finally said, "you want me to believe that The Queen of England has been tooling around America in the back seat of a military jet, helping the RAF with publicity at air shows?" The patrolman's eyes narrowed as he looked at The Queen. "I'm afraid I can't buy that, Ma'am," he earnestly said.

"I can vouch for her!" Ellen June suddenly said while walking over to Elizabeth. "I'm with the government," she added.

Jon and his father looked at each other with raised eyebrows.

"And who are you Ma'am?" The officer inquired as he glanced at Jon's wife.

"Ellen June Jung," she calmly replied.

"Can I see some identification?" The patrolman asked.

"Sure," Ellen said. She walked over to a desk and opened a hidden compartment in the top drawer. Without looking at the business size card that had been placed there, she picked it up, returned to the officer and handed it to him.

The lawman scrutinized the ID. It read:

Ellen June Jung
Company Snoop
Surveillance Division
I'm Watching You!

After looking over the ID, the officer held up the card and asked, "Is this for real?"

"Yes," Ellen June replied. "It has the government logo on it."

The patrolman checked the front and the back of the ID and then asked, "Where?"

Reaching for the card Ellen said, "May I?"

Handing the ID back, the officer said, "Please do."

Ellen June looked closely at the card. "Where the heck did this come from?" She said. "This isn't my ID!" Ellen looked over at her father-in-law. He had a slight smile on his face.

Samuel stepped forward and said, "Can I speak with you in private, Officer?"

The patrolman waved him closer, and as Samuel passed Ellen June he whispered, "Fooled them!"

The elder Jung took hold of the officer's arm and moved him further out onto the porch. The two could be seen from the living room but not heard. Samuel reached into his pocket, took out his wallet, and pulled out his Company credentials, which showed him to be a bona fide agent.

As Jon's father talked to the patrol officer, they both looked over at Ellen. Samuel pointed his index finger at his head and made a circular motion, indicating that Ellen June, perhaps, was not all there. They talked for a few more minutes, then the officer shook Samuel's hand, turned and departed.

As Samuel was walking towards the front door, a military motorcycle with sidecar, driven by Corporal Hawkins, pulled up and parked in front of the house. "I believe your ride is here, Your Grace," Samuel said to the monarch.

"Honestly," Elizabeth responded when she saw the motorcycle, "could the RAF possibly have picked any shoddier transportation?"

"Your Majesty!" Hawkins said upon seeing The Queen as he approached. "I'm here to take you back to the airbase."

"Ever faithful, Corporal Hawkins!" The Queen said. "What would I ever do without you?"

The Royal Marine smiled at Her Royal Highness, and then bowed.

"By the way, Hawkins, how did you know where to locate me?"

Before the corporal could respond, Samuel said, "I took the liberty of contacting the head of your security team while you and Ellen were in the kitchen, Your Grace."

"On top of everything, as usual, Samuel!" Elizabeth said. "Thank you!"

Samuel bowed and said, "Your servant."

Turning to the corporal, The Queen, chiding the young man a bit said, "Tell me, Hawkins, is this the best vehicle that you could find to collect the Queen of England?"

"Well, Ma'am," the Royal Marine replied, slightly embarrassed, "it was either the motorcycle and sidecar, or a funeral coach."

Elizabeth smiled warmly at the young man and said, "Considering where we are at the moment, the latter might have been a better choice!"

Corporal Hawkins bowed in acknowledgment and then said, "The base commander said he'd arrange to pick up the car at another time."

"Nonsense!" Elizabeth replied. "Richard, here, can drive the car back to the base. Would you like that, Son?"

Enthusiastically, Richie responded, "Yes, Ma'am!"

Holding the car keys out to the young man at arm's length, The Queen then quickly withdrew them, saying, "Of course, that's if it's OK with your father."

Richie looked at his dad and pleaded, saying, "Please!"

Jon hesitated a moment, then replied, "OK." He jokingly added, "But, keep it under 100!"

"This is so bitchin'!" Richie exclaimed.

"Richie! Your language! The Queen!" Ellen scolded.

"It's just an expression, Dear," Elizabeth said, to which she added, "Oh, the exuberance of youth!"

Richie ran up to The Queen and was handed the car keys. "Thank you, Your Grace."

"My pleasure," she replied.

The young man bolted out to the car with eager anticipation. Jon, now serious said, "Richie, under 100!" He added, "I mean it!"

When the young man got into the sports car and started the engine, its entire 400 horsepower already sounded as if it was straining to be let loose before the parking brake was even released. As Richie popped the clutched and the car rapidly accelerated away, Jon said, "Maybe that wasn't such a good idea."

Corporal Hawkins was somewhat envious of the youth as he watched the red sports car pull away, but as the car disappeared from sight, he immediately became mindful of his duty to The Queen. "Your Grace," the Royal Marine said directly, "we must get back to the base shortly. The Red Arrows are having a banquet tonight in your honor. They'll be serving haggis!"

Elizabeth recoiled slightly at the thought of the dish. "If ever I decide to abdicate the throne," she said, "it will probably be because I can't face another meal featuring haggis!"

The corporal resisted looking over at the monarch, and wisely remained silent.

"Well," Elizabeth said, "there' no putting off the inevitable!"

Retrieving a pair of leather gloves from her flight suit, she told the marine, "We better get moving, Corporal."

"Yes, Ma'am!" Hawkins replied. "If you would be kind enough to step over to the sidecar. . . ,"

The Queen interrupted. "No, Hawkins," she said with resolve. "You're in the sidecar. I'm driving!"

"But, Your Grace!" The corporal protested.

"Hawkins!" Elizabeth said after holding up her hand to halt any further insurrection. "Get in, hold on, and shut up!"

"Yes, Your Grace," the Royal Marine replied, in total obedience.

"Now," The Queen said, holding her hand out as Hawkins sat down, "give me the key!"

Complying with the monarch's demand, the corporal passed over the key. Placing it in the ignition and then kick starting the engine, The Queen said, "I'm going to enjoy this!" The Royal Marine, white as a sheet, obviously wasn't looking forward to the journey with the same anticipation. Glancing at the marine The Queen said, "Relax Corporal and breath! I'm in complete control!" Adjusting her aviator sunglasses, Elizabeth looked over to the front door where Ellen, Jon, and Samuel had gathered. "Goodbye, all," she said as she expertly and smoothly pulled away on the motorcycle.

The Jungs waved goodbye to The Queen and her military escort.

"Capable woman," Samuel said.

"That she is," Jon concurred.

The three stepped back from the doorway, and Jon shut the door.

"Speaking of capable women," Samuel said, "why don't we sit down and have a little talk."

Jon took Ellen's hand as they approached the couch and sat down. Samuel, following behind them, took his place next to Ellen. Looking at his father Jon said, "Why don't you start?"

Samuel turned to his daughter-in-law and smiled. "In many ways, Ellen, you are very intelligent and adept," he said. "We're not sure how involved you are with this Company program to keep tabs on its agents through the use of hired casual informants. We're not even sure how extensive the program is or how long it's been in operation, but we have resources to find out."

"What we do know, however," Jon said, then adding his own concerns, "is that we don't want you to be placed in danger because you know too much."

Samuel then spoke. "Since you are a capable woman, there might be an opportunity for you to join the ranks of The Company legitimately."

"I thought I already had," Ellen June replied. "The ID I was issued had a logo, and everything."

"That wasn't a logo," Jon said, holding up the card that Ellen thought she had given to the patrol officer earlier, "that was a smiley face!"

Looking at the ID in Jon's hand, Ellen started to giggle, "So it is," she said.

"Who gave that to you?" Samuel inquired.

"That guy named Fred," Ellen June replied.

"Well," Jon told her, "*that guy* had no authority to issue any kind of ID on his own. If you actually were employed by The Company, you would have been issued official credentials. We'll have to do something about Fred."

"It won't be anything bad, will it?" Ellen asked.

"No, we'll just have him transferred to Alaska, or Cleveland, or someplace worse," Samuel replied with a smile.

Ellen and Jon both smiled at the thought.

"So," Samuel finally said to Ellen, "do you want to come on board?"

"We'll be right at your side to help you along," Jon quickly added.

"Well," Ellen June said, "I always thought I could be more than a housewife . . . ,"

Jon smiled at his wife and asked, "Is that a yes, then?"

"That's a yes," Ellen responded.

Jon and Ellen hugged each other and then glanced over to Jon's father, who looked concerned.

"Does this mean that you won't be making cookies for me anymore?" Sammy asked.

"No, Dad," Ellen said. "I'll still be baking your cookies."

"Excellent," Samuel said, with a glowing smile.

Just then, there was a knock at the front door.

"Now what?" Ellen June uttered, not expecting another visitor.

"I'll get it," Jon said, letting out a sigh as he got off the couch.

When he went to the door and opened it, he was surprised to see The Queen standing on the porch.

"Your Grace?" Jon said, wondering why the monarch may have returned.

"Oh! Hello again, Jon," Elizabeth said, obviously embarrassed. "I knew I should have gone before I left, but . . . , would you mind if I used your loo?"

Aftermath

In 1985, President Ronald Reagan awarded Ellen June Jung the Presidential Medal of Freedom for twenty years of dedicated service to the country. During that period, Ellen also continued to make pickled watermelon rind, and bake cookies.

Jon Jung retired, also in 1985, and began playing golf to give him something to do. He abandoned his efforts to incorporate part of an eighteen hole golf course into the cemetery, because the grave markers proved too much of a hindrance to the game. He now golfs at the municipal golf course five days a week.

Samuel Jung, likewise in 1985, was looking forward to his 100th birthday, only a couple of years away. He attributed his long life to, well, you guessed it - Cookies!

Richard Jung, by 1985, was firmly established in a career working in government intelligence, and would eventually become the station chief of a foreign mission in the Middle East. After high school, he and Susan went their separate ways, with Susan traveling to Africa to become a Christian missionary.

Finally, in 1985, Susan's mother had been missing for more than twenty years. She would never be seen or heard from again.

You Just Can't Make Up This Stuff!

The information on the much traveled corpse of Evita came from:

Cristin Conger, <u>Why did it take more than 20 years to bury Eva Peron?</u>
http: www.howstuffworks.com

Steve Myall, <u>Carted thousands of miles and kept on her husband's dinner table: How the remarkable story of Evita carried on after her death.</u>
http:www.mirror.co.uk

The story of the "Dilbert Dunker" was frequently related by the late, irrepressible, Leonard "Komo" Komisarik, a family friend. No one could possibly tell it better.

The quote, "What I don't know is what I don't know", was a response from a government spokesperson to a question on a national security issue. Heard on a CBS radio news broadcast on Friday, October 3, 2014. It was too good to pass up!

Finally, the item about the young man that wanted to throw himself out of a moving pickup truck into a cactus was from a featured segment on the "World's Dumbest . . . . " television broadcast.

For errors and omissions submit to Documents Division Internal Review, Langley, VA